Pulphouse
FICTION MAGAZINE

Issue Thirty-Four

Magazine Editor
Dean Wesley Smith

A WMG Publishing Magazine

Pulphouse Fiction Magazine Issue #34
Published by WMG Publishing Inc.
Cover and interior design copyright © 2024 WMG Publishing Inc.
Cover art copyright © lightsource | Depositphotos
Small creature we call Thumper copyright © beutoszig | Depositphotos

Pulphouse

FICTION MAGAZINE

TABLE OF CONTENTS

Pulphouse Fiction Magazine
A WMG Publishing Magazine

Editor	*Executive Editor*	*Director of Operations*
Dean Wesley Smith	Kristine Kathryn Rusch	Stephanie Writt

FROM THE EDITOR'S DESK
SUPERSTITIOUS

This October, as you read this, I will be wrapped in layers of Bubble Wrap, taking food through a straw, and just trying not to move. Well, not really, but a part of me wants to do that.

You see, in October 2022, I woke one fine October morning with a bad infection in my only good eye. I was basically blind for the rest of the year and the infection finally left after six months giving me about 70% of my vision back.

I am fine and learning to live with the new vision.

Then in October of 2023, I was feeling good, running in a 5K charity run with the leaders, forgot about my newly limited vision, tripped on a curb, and smashed up my shoulder as I tried to roll into the fall on the concrete.

New titanium shoulder and nine months of physical therapy later, I am fine. (But I still find it interesting that because of my age, everyone in the hospital assumed I had fallen reaching for the remote. Not kidding.)

So I think you can see why October this year scares me more than ghosts or children wearing Donald Trump masks trick-or-treating. (Does Bubble Wrap ward off ghosts?)

As things happen in publishing, I am writing this introduction in August, so we shall see.

One of the many things I do love about October is the weather, which for Vegas is flat perfect. Kris and I start walking everywhere in October, and I still plan on participating in the charity fun runs. More than likely walking. At 74 my running full speed days are behind me.

And I also love the fiction that focuses on Halloween and ghosts and so on. Got a few of those stories in this issue, including a brand-new original Halloween story by Kristine Kathryn Rusch.

So I hope you enjoy the read and the wonderful fall

month. I will see you on the other side if my luck holds and the Bubble Wrap does its job.

DEAN WESLEY SMITH
LAS VEGAS, NEVADA

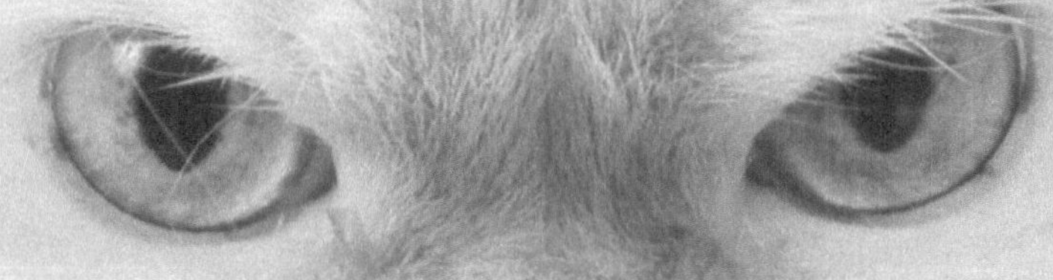

PULPHOUSE KITTY SAYS:
SUBSCRIBE
ebook or paperback
pulphousemagazine.com
Pulphouse
FICTION MAGAZINE

KRISTINE KATHRYN RUSCH

Kristine Kathryn Rusch is a New York Times *and* USA Today *bestselling writer and maybe the most award-winning and prolific writer working today. She has won more awards in science fiction and mystery than just about anyone alive and she is the only person to win the Hugo Award for her writing as well as her editing.*

This story ended up here when Kris was passing by my office and I casually asked, "Got a Halloween story for the October issue?"

She said, "Sure." And a minute later the story popped into my in-box and it is perfect for this October issue. So perfect, I made it the featured story.

So here it is, leading off the issue. Enjoy.

You can find out a lot more about Kris's work at her publisher, WMG Publishing Inc. wmgbooks.com or her website kriswrites.com.

BLAZING BLUE

KRISTINE KATHRYN RUSCH

Emily Hayes had a weakness for Halloween stores. She loved Halloween stuff much more than Christmas stuff or even pretty non-holiday items. She didn't buy much because up until a month or two ago, she hadn't had enough room, but at Halloween she always got herself a new mug or a scarf or something small and fun.

So when she saw the black-and-orange electronic sign flashing above the latest pop-up store in the only strip mall in this part of Seavy Village, she promised herself a stop on the way home.

Home was now a dilapidated old house on the top of a hill about five blocks from here. She wouldn't have to drive to the pop-up at all if she didn't want to, but she had some supplies to get from the hardware store, things she had to hold and consider, instead of ordering them online.

After more than a decade of online shopping, it felt weird to go to a store to get things. But she'd learned, after she had moved into Aunt Maisey's house, that there was nothing standard about it. Measurements didn't help. Photographs didn't work. Trying to find the elusive missing bolt that would work in that particular screw hole required a bolt from a nearby screw hole and an expert who would eyeball it and tell her what, exactly, she was missing.

And she was missing a lot.

She had thought she would love living on the coast. That was one of the reasons she had taken on the house instead of selling it like the broker wanted her to do.

Another reason was that the house had been in the family for generations. Emily was the only one left, and losing the house felt like losing another close family member. She felt like she would betray everyone if she let it go.

She knew the arguments: Amber, her best friend, had earned the right to be blunt with her since they'd known each other since that first scary day of kindergarten, and Amber often used that right. She did when she heard Emily's reason for keeping the house.

You <u>can't</u> let them down, Amber had said. They're <u>dead</u>.

Emily knew that, but she didn't know that. She could feel the family near her, judging her sometimes, encouraging her other times. There was history that she didn't want to let go of, and memories that only resided in that house on the hill, and lots and lots of love that might just vanish if she let it all go.

Moving into the house and fixing it up felt like a compulsion, but not one she should fight. One she needed to give into, so she had.

She had a lot of money saved from the hated IT job, and then she learned that Aunt Maisey had been one of those people who never spent a dime on herself. The money in the Maisey estate was staggering—and that was her lawyer's term—but finding it all was proving difficult.

Every yellowed stack of papers that Emily found in the various rooms of the house had mysterious envelopes from dozens of different banks. If this had been a digital trail, she could have conquered it in a heartbeat, but Aunt Maisey had been stubbornly analog.

Some days, Emily loved the challenge.

Other days, like today, she wanted to return to Portland and live her old frustrating little life at the beck and call of executives who thought computers worked better when you pounded the mouse against the keyboard in frustration.

That memory made her feel better, and so did the black-and orange electronic sign above the pop-up store after her hour-plus with Mr. Wineglass at the hardware store. At first, the sign was just a blur of Halloween color against the very dark and stormy sky. The peeks of the ocean she got between the buildings was just as black and gray as the sky, but had the added benefit of huge, white, foam-covered waves.

No matter what the weather app on her watch said, the storm that was hovering offshore was going to be a big one.

Aunt Maisey always said the ocean had a lot of secrets, but it told no lies. So when it was roiling with anger at an impending storm, Aunt Maisey would say, everyone had better listen.

Emily had listened, days ago, when the surfers showed up. They liked to chase big waves, and their computer models had predicted gigantic waves here at the end of October. Big waves came from big storms, often off shore. But she had looked up the month-long weather forecast, looked at the storm patterns, and thought that the surfers had been both right and wrong: right in that there would be some really big waves; wrong in that the waves would be the only thing to hit the coast.

So she had prepared.

She had been coming to the coast off and on ever since she had been a child, and she knew that there was nothing more fragile than electricity during a powerful coastal windstorm. She was a woman who needed electricity like she needed air, so she bought a huge generator and had it professionally installed.

Then she added some food to a secondary fridge, made sure there were a lot of bags of ice in the freezer, and bought extra battery powered lights. She had snacks and a couple of iPads charged and ready to go with movies if she needed the distraction.

She also had a guy come out and clean up the house's five

fireplaces. She bought a cord of wood and had it placed inside the garage where Aunt Maisey had (stupidly) kept the original generator, which the new generator guys kindly dragged away to the dump.

Emily would have done all of this work anyway, but the ocean and its warnings had given her an excuse to do it all immediately. She had told Amber on the phone that she was simply getting ready for a coastal winter, because she didn't want to discuss the feeling that she'd been carrying around since she first saw the waves growing:

She felt like this storm was going to be consequential.

She just didn't know what that meant yet.

The blur of orange and black soon resolved itself with a bit of green. The sign read Halloween Pop-up in neon orange letters, with black images behind it. A digital green frog would hop across the bottom, and stop to look at the road before hopping to the other end of the sign. The frog wore a pointed witch's cap and, at the far end of the sign, climbed onto a broomstick and flew away.

It was a nice piece of engineering that she hoped would survive the storm. She knew that no previous storm had brought down that sign, because in the year before her death, Aunt Maisey had complained about it in letters and postcards, saying that it ruined her view.

Emily couldn't even see the sign from the house. She had no idea what view Aunt Maisey had been referring to, but it hadn't been the one from the ocean- and 101-facing windows.

Emily liked this sign. Maybe Aunt Maisey had meant that the sign blocked her view from the road when she drove, and it did do that. It hid some of the cliffside caves that were sometimes visible when the tide was down.

Not that it mattered. Aunt Maisey was gone and Emily loved the sign. She wasn't sure she'd like the next sign for the next pop-up, but this one actually made her happy.

And as she clocked that emotion, she realized she hadn't felt this kind of happy for a very long time.

She pulled into the ancient strip mall's parking lot just as the rain began. She knew from hard experience to park on the 101 side of the lot away from the stores, not because of other cars, but because in a heavy rain, the store side of the parking area became a lake.

The sidewalk had been raised two feet years ago so that the water wouldn't slide into the stores, but that just meant that the lake grew bigger when the storms were particularly fierce.

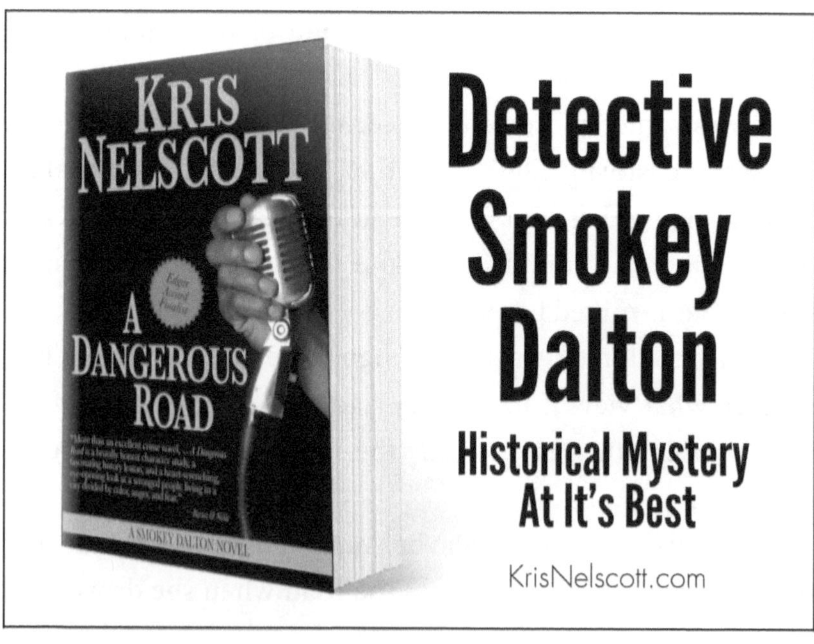

This storm was going to be fierce.

Hers was the only car in the front lot. The usual decrepit coastal cars were on the employee parking side, along with a bright blue truck that was so shiny it looked like it was volunteering to become the salt air's next victim.

She wrapped her Gore-Tex coat around her middle, pulled up the hood, and got out of the car, sprinting across the parking lot as the rain turned from moody to pelting.

The pop-up was in the very middle of the strip mall, squished between a rather seedy wine shop and an antique store that was antique in name only. The center storefront was impossible to rent permanently because it was so small. It didn't have a back, because the back area was used for the ridiculous turret that rose above the top of the entire mall.

The owners had gone to a series of pop-ups and advertised the space in the Willamette Valley as a test market— Want to see if your store has coastal possibilities? Look no farther than Seavy Village's Castle Mall...

She hadn't gone into the previous pop-up even though it had Closing Sale! signs plastered everywhere when she moved in. She'd peered in the tiny windows and seen some rather cheap jewelry and decided that the place just wasn't for her.

This pop-up was. As she got closer, she saw some lovely old posters pasted against the glass of windows, and beneath them, on the display shelf, all kinds of candy lost in the fake bright green grass that she always associated with Easter, not Halloween.

The front of the door was covered with a die-cut of a witch hat, and a small frog in the corner. That frog was the same frog as the one on the electronic sign. Apparently, this place had a mascot.

She pushed the door open, slid inside, and stopped immediately.

It wasn't what she expected.

The interior was a little too dark and smelled of old paper and mildew. Rather like the smell of a library in a very old building. The darkness didn't just come from the incoming storm. The covered windows kept the light out (except along the edges) and the single overhead light above the door was a weak fluorescent that had brown water damage around its ballasts.

In front of her was a waterfall display with costumes sealed in packages. She had expected costumes, but she had expected them to hang on racks, with the masks on a separate shelf, all with their own packaging and instructions. These costumes were all-in-one and the packaging looked old, with a cellophane opening that showed the mask, surrounded by some witchy art designed for children. Underneath all of them were the words complete with ventilated mask!

She would have hoped that the masks would be ventilated. People had to breathe somehow.

Her heart rate increased slightly, and she felt the need to move away from the shelf. It took a moment to realize why. Two clown masks bookended the upper row—the first with a white face and downturned features and the second vaguely female, with blond curls and a smile revealing pointed teeth.

She hated clowns so, she supposed, that would make them appropriate as a Halloween costume. But not appropriate for her. She also disapproved of the politican masks she saw every year at Walmart or the celebrity glue-ons that always looked somewhat wrong to her. They were just not fun.

She slipped around the waterfall shelf, careful not to let her Gore-Tex coat drip on anything, and found herself in a wonderland of stuff she had never seen before—all lit by lights with Halloween designs. Witches glowed darkly, pumpkins added some red, and black cats would send laser-like white light out of their eyes.

The effect was almost comforting, as if the entire world had become a commercial (but ancient) Halloween just for a dark and gloomy afternoon. A couple of the lamps had fake flickering fire in their bases. One lamp, placed in the center of a table littered with cards and packaged candy, had a shade that rotated and cast shadows on the tiny paper wall behind it.

She walked over to that table, watching as a 1950s silhouette of a child ran ahead of a group of goblins and ghosts and ghouls. The way the shadows moved, it almost looked like a play—that poor silhouetted child forever trapped in a moment of escape.

"That," said a deep male voice behind her, "was one of my mother's favorites."

Emily jumped. She hadn't heard anyone approach. She knew she couldn't be alone in here, but it had felt like she was, even for just a moment.

She turned around slowly, still clutching the Gore-tex, her fingers tight against the zipper.

A tall man with the broadest shoulders she'd seen outside of professional sports stood a few feet behind her, near a table with lace embroidery done in orange and black. His black hair curled over his forehead. Some silver threaded through it, changing color as the lights around him changed as well.

He had high cheekbones and a pointed chin that somehow looked right on him. His blue eyes were electric. She felt like she could stare at them for hours.

"I'm sorry," he said. "I didn't mean to startle you."

She let out a small sigh. No chance she could deny the startle, and now she was feeling a bit dumb.

"It's all right," she said. "I, um, just didn't hear you."

"Yeah, the wind is starting to whistle," he said.

And now that he mentioned it, she could hear it, the wind almost singing as it found the gaps in the old building's frame.

"We're due for a heck of a storm," she said. "I hope the roof here is sound."

"Oh, I checked before I rented the place," he said. "I was more worried that electronic sign would crash through the beams. The coast isn't known for its building codes."

"Especially when this place was built," she said.

"Especially then." His smile widened. He had a slightly crooked tooth up front, which eased the perfection of his features and made him seem just a bit less perfect. "Well, I'll leave you to it."

"Thanks," she said, not wanting him to go, but she didn't want to say that. He wasn't really leaving. He was walking to a far corner of the store where a computer sat on a built-in counter. Her old IT eye caught the computer's plug going directly into the wall.

She walked over. "Do you have a surge protector?" she asked, gesturing at the cord. "Power goes out easily here."

"I'd been meaning to get one," he said. "Just haven't gotten around to it. I guess I'll have to hope nothing happens today and make getting one a priority tomorrow."

That wouldn't work, but she didn't say that. She knew how to handle people who simply did not understand the impact of brown-outs and complete blackouts on their computers.

"I have one in my car," she said. "I'll get it for you."

"No, that's okay," he said, but she was already heading for the door. She pushed it open.

The wind was howling now, and the rain pelting so hard that it hit the concrete sidewalk and then bounced upward. The lake in the lot was starting to form.

She jumped over it and went to her car. In the back, she always kept extra supplies—batteries, surge protectors, and a wide variety of phone chargers. It had been a habit she developed at the old job, particularly when the original boss had proven too cheap to buy the right equipment in the first place. She would buy it and then she would bill him as expenses.

The habit had stuck, but she had never gotten around to billing these.

She hit the remote as she crossed the lot, and her car beeped its greeting before releasing the trunk. It started to come up in the wind, but the wind pushed it down. She caught the edge before it slammed shut.

She held it open, grabbed two surge protectors and some actual flashlights before easing it down.

Then she sprinted across the parking lot again, jumping the growing lake.

The gorgeous man stood at the open door, watching her, an expression of bemusement on his face.

"Do you come prepared for everything?" he asked.

"No," she said. "I just have this because of my old job. If I came prepared for everything, I'd have tarps for you in case the roof leaks. Because the stuff you have inside is lovely."

"I have the tarps," he said, standing back. "And yes, everything is lovely or scary or fun."

Only he didn't sound enthusiastic about it. He also didn't strike her as the kind of person who collected Halloween memorabilia. If she had to guess—and she knew it was based on a mental cliché—she would have thought this place was owned either by an elderly woman or a 30-something geeky collector who stood too close as he described the provenance of each item.

This man just seemed out of place in both the small space and among all the stuff. What had he said to her? That the rotating lamp was his mother's favorite.

Emily stepped inside. "I've been coming to the coast since

I was a kid," she said. "When they tell you this is going to be a big storm, you have to believe them."

"I've done the same," he said, "and I didn't hear that this one was going to be big."

She half-opened her mouth to contradict him and then realized most people didn't listen to the surfers. She did.

"Trust me," she said, "it's already raining too hard for anyone to stop here today on a whim. Let's unplug the fancy stuff like that really nifty lamp that your mother loved and make sure that your computer is protected."

He looked around, like he was reluctant to change anything. Then he said, "Probably sensible," and reached around her for a very plain (and very old) light switch.

Her tech intuition tingled. No one had examined the electrical system of this building in a very long time.

The lights overhead flickered, coating everything in a whitish brown light that came from more damaged fluorescents. She looked up at them.

"You sure this place doesn't leak?" she asked.

"Not that sure," he said. "I'll get the tarps."

She nodded and went to the back. The electrical outlet had a two places to plug in but was so old that it only had one ground.

"I need you to shut down the computer," she said, setting the largest surge protector on the uneven wooden plank floor.

The man came over and went around the counter, grabbing the mouse in his long fingers. For a moment, she flashed back on all of those executives who banged their own mouse around like it was misbehaving. Then she looked away as she scanned the area for more things to plug into the protector.

She didn't see a lot. This place was as analog as her Aunt Maisey's house. With the overheads on, pretty much everything else could be unplugged.

"Okay, it's off," the man said from behind her. She walked to the counter. He was standing by the computer. He held out a hand. "I'm Walker, by the way."

She took it. His fingers were warm, but as they wrapped around her hand, they sent a shiver through her.

"Emily," she said.

And because her reaction embarrassed her, she bent down and unplugged the computer. She plugged in the surge protector and then plugged the computer into it.

"You can turn it back on now," she said.

"I'm going to leave it off for the moment. Let's just leave it all unplugged right now, what do you say?" He was making his way out from behind the counter as he spoke, unplugging some of the pretty lights.

"I think that's a plan," she said.

"What do I owe you for that protector?" he asked.

"Oh, I don't know," she said. "A coffee maybe, on a day when a storm's not brewing."

"Deal," he said and smiled at her. That warmth trickled through her again. This man was amazing.

"Let me help you unplug everything," she said.

He grabbed two large battery operated lights from behind the counter, and he held them up. "See?" he said. "I'm not entirely unprepared."

She laughed and made her way to the tables with the

lovely lace tops. They all had embroidered witches and goblins in them and were mostly black or orange, but they also had a touch of green.

"This frog," she said, "it strikes me as someone's signature."

"My mom's," he said. "She made the lacework and did some of the art."

He sounded both proud and sad.

"It's gorgeous," she said. "How much are they?"

Because it was time to make Aunt Maisey's house her own, and what would be better but some large black doilies with witches on them.

"Those aren't for sale," he said. "Mom collected Halloween stuff, and I have no need of that, but her work? It's staying with me. I just thought it would be nice to have it here as part of the display."

Something in his tone caught her. "Past tense," she said.

"Yeah," he said. "She died in February. It took me a while to figure out what to do with the collectibles."

Collectibles. That would be an issue for Emily too, at some point. Not yet thought.

She unplugged the last lamp. With its orange light gone, the store now looked like a tiny antiques shop, bad lighting and tables filled with random items. Some of the magic had left.

She started to make her way to the back to grab a tarp when she bumped one of the tables. It wobbled and she had to grab the lamp so that it wouldn't fall. She gripped the edge of the table, steadying it, and accidentally pulled off a piece of paper.

Then she realized it wasn't paper but cardstock. She turned it over and saw a familiar drawing.

It showed the comfortable front of a fireplace, cauldron over a blazing fire, a red wooden stool on the right side. Cast against the wall was the shadowy silhouette of a traditional witch, complete with broomstick and pointed hat.

Something Emily had noticed before, but had never really paid attention to, was the frog, sitting beneath the stool and peering with great curiosity at the shadow of the witch.

Aunt Maisey had one of these cards. It sat on top of a pile that Emily hadn't sorted through yet. She had thought that maybe she should frame it for her own Halloween collection, miniscule as it was.

"What's this?" she asked.

"I don't know exactly," Walker said. "It's a little card my mother drew up. Read the inside."

Emily hadn't realized that it was a card. She had to slide a fingernail along the edge to open it. There, in a beautiful scrawl, was this poem:

> When lights burn low with blazes blue
> And witches weave a charm
> I'll long for someone just like you
> To keep me from all harm

"Oh, wow," she said. "That's pretty. How many of these did she make?"

"To my knowledge," Walker said, "that's the only one."

"It's not," Emily said. "My aunt Maisey had one."

He looked at her, a frown creasing his forehead.

And then the lights went out.

———

There was never a moment of complete darkness, although it seemed that way. In the seconds it took Emily's eyes to adjust, she felt like everything had changed, but she didn't know why.

Then the light from the battery operated lamps came on—or maybe she just noticed that as well.

Walker had set one on the counter and one on a middle table.

"I think we better continue covering everything," Emily said as she got her voice back. She set the card on the table she had bumped, and turned on one of her flashlights.

The wind was howling now, the whistles piercing. The rain pelting the windows sounded like rocks trying to smash the glass.

"I think you're right," he said.

Together they spread half a dozen tarps over his mother's collection. When they were done, it looked like they had created a series of little mountains that rose and fell in the darkness.

"It's going to get cold in here," Emily said.

"Yeah." He looked around. "I think everything's unplugged. How long do you think this'll last?"

"Four years ago, when I was here over Christmas, we were out of power for five days."

"Yikes!" he said. "Seriously?"

"Yeah," she said. "But Aunt Maisey says they fixed the infrastructure. So now I think it might be shorter. Depends if the power's out in the valley. If so, we're an afterthought."

He sighed and shook his head. "Well, this'll be fun," he said.

"It might be." She smiled at him. "I have a generator. We can go there."

He peered at her in surprise. And honestly, she was a bit surprised herself. She normally didn't invite strange men to her house, especially on such short acquaintance. But it felt like she had known him forever.

"You sure?" he asked. "Because I could go to my mom's. There's a fireplace."

"I have five," she said.

"Now, you're just making fun of me," he said.

"No," she said. "My aunt Maisey left me her house. It's the big one on the hill. I can show you the card."

"Does it have a frog, your card?" he asked.

Emily nodded.

Then he let out a small sigh. "Before you do, I should probably tell you something."

"What's that?" Emily asked.

He squared his shoulders and then gave her an uncomfortable half-smile. "My mom only gave her artwork to family."

Emily frowned. She didn't understand at all. "Are you saying we're related? Because I can assure you we're not. I did the family tree-thing a few years ago—"

"No," he said, and gave her a thin smile. "My mom—um—she fell in love before my dad."

Emily froze. Suddenly all of her senses were alive. The howl of the wind, the pulsating darkness outside, the harsh light from the battery-operated lamps, all seemed even more potent.

"She used to tell us that sometimes young love doesn't work out," he said.

"Us?"

"Me and my sisters." He smiled again, but it wasn't a real smile. It was the kind people got when they were lost in a memory. "I didn't think a lot about it until I cleaned out the attic of the Portland house. There were letters from a woman named Maisey, and it didn't take me long to realize…"

"That they were love letters," Emily said.

He nodded.

"And that poem," he said. "My mom didn't write it. Maisey did. In the good-bye letter."

Emily let out a breath, remembering some of the letters and postcards she had gotten in the past year.

> *Em, I met someone. Or I should say, re-met someone. Maybe the next time you're here, we can all get together…*

And then, a month or so later:

> *You know the problem with getting old? Everything is finite. Even life. If you fall in love, Em, don't wait too long. Life and love are to be grabbed, or they might disappear forever.*

"Your mom died in February?" she asked.

"Yeah," he said.

February. When she had gotten that very sad letter from Aunt Maisey. Emily had come to the coast for the weekend over Valentine's and spent most of it, holding her sobbing aunt, who had said only that an old and dear friend had passed away.

Sometimes one doesn't get the second chance after all, Aunt Maisey had said—cryptically at the time.

"Oh, my," Emily said.

"And your aunt is gone now too?" he asked.

She nodded. "It all makes sense now. I think she died of a broken heart."

They looked at each other.

"Witches," Emily said after a moment. "They're all over your mom's work."

"Yeah," he said. "And frogs."

She was going to ignore the frog for a moment.

"Witches," she said again. "Aunt Maisey always said they were symbolic of the kind of women who didn't fit in."

She and Walker stared at each other. There was nothing to say, not right now. Emily wished she had known earlier because she would have...what? She had no idea.

Her aunt Maisey was of a different generation, one in which certain behaviors were "normal" and others were not. One that had laws to enforce such notions of "normality" and prevent people who truly loved each other from having futures together.

Emily swallowed hard. She would not cry in front of a

man she had just met, no matter how kind he seemed. But in this dim light, it seemed like his eyes were damp too.

"Tell you what," she said. "Come to my place. I'll make us some hot cocoa and if you can have alcohol, we'll add a little rum. Then we'll toast them—your mom and my aunt."

He looked uncertain.

"I have witch mugs," she said.

He laughed. "How can anyone turn that down?" he said. He grabbed a useless leather jacket off a chair behind the counter.

"That'll get ruined," she said.

"Ah, it's seen coastal winters before," he said. "Besides, my truck is just outside the door."

"The blue one?" she asked.

"Yeah, why?" he said.

"Well…" she said slowly, "it looks about as coastal as your coat."

He laughed. "Give it time," he said.

"I'll wait for you on the road," she said. "You can follow me up to the house."

"Deal. I'll lock up."

She nodded, then headed to the door. He opened it.

The rain wasn't individual drops any longer. It looked like a waterfall pouring out of the sky.

"Tell you what," he said. "I'll drive you home and when it lets up, I'll bring you back to your car."

"Or I can walk," she said. "It's only a few blocks away."

He pushed the door closed and locked it. Then he led her through the darkened store to the back. A side door she hadn't even noticed opened into a narrow hallway that smelled damp. She didn't say anything, though.

The other thing she knew about these storms was that they caused changes. But it was better not to examine those changes while they were happening. Better to wait until the sun came out again because everything was clearer in the sunlight.

He locked the second door to the store, then led her down the hallway to another door that opened onto the employee parking lot. He was right: his truck was only two yards away —at least the driver's side.

He sprinted first and she followed, climbing inside after he unlocked it. Driving in the rain would be a challenge, but then everything was here.

Sometimes people didn't conquer a challenge, but sometimes they did.

Her aunt Maisey and Walker's mother never really got a chance. But Emily had learned one thing: she had been right about the love in that house. It held the memories of a relationship that wasn't over yet—and maybe never would be.

She smiled at Walker. She liked him. And trusted him. If nothing else, they'd have a nice stormy afternoon talking about witches and frogs and lost loves.

Or maybe they'd live out the truth of that poem—sitting by a blazing blue fire, with someone who could keep them from all harm.

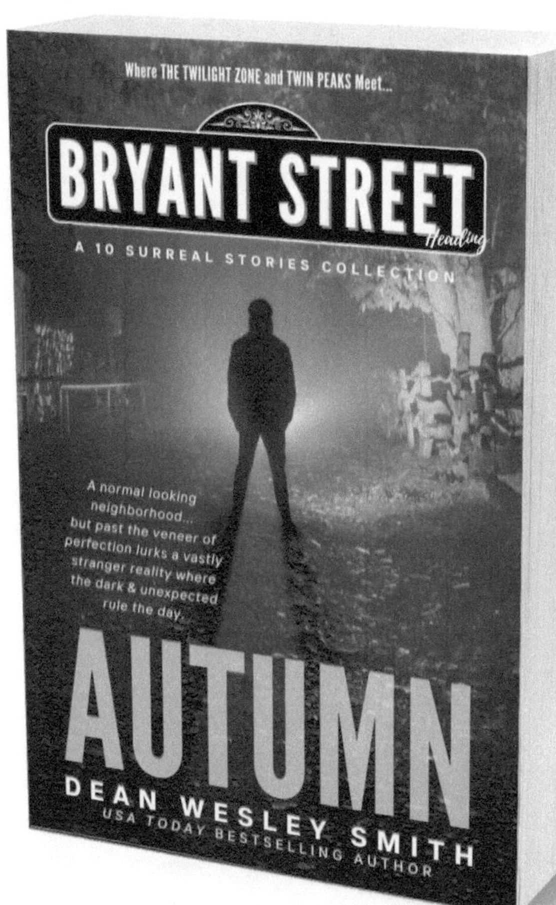

Where
THE TWILIGHT ZONE
Lives...

wmgbooks.com

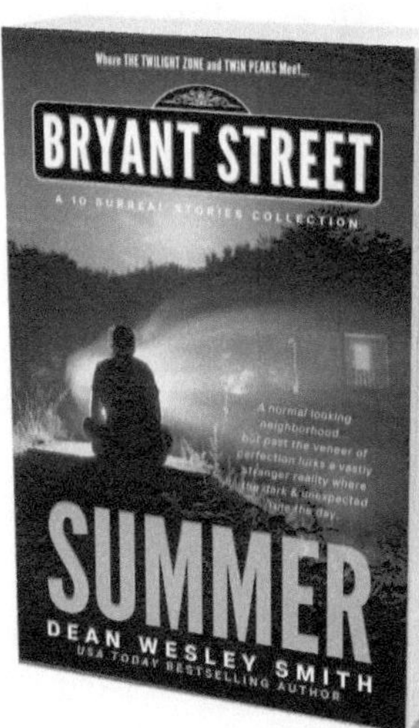

R.W. WALLACE

R. W. Wallace returns to these pages with this story in a series of wonderful fantasy mystery stories that have been and will be in many issues of this magazine.

These stories are not like any standard mystery. The detective is a ghost, limited to his own cemetery helping other ghosts move on by solving their problems. In other words, the detective is locked in a confined space with no tools, trying to help a victim discover what happened to them.

A wonderful series that I am lucky enough to run in this magazine. And for even more of her work, check out her website at rwwallace.com.

DULL EXPECTATIONS

R.W. WALLACE

Cemeteries are mostly associated with death, human mortality, and loss. When someone says the word, we think of dark and stormy nights, squealing hinges, and moaning ghosts. Serial killers using it as their hunting ground, or junkies as a place to get high in peace. There's no lack of stories, be they on screen or on paper, to support these beliefs.

After spending thirty years haunting this specific cemetery, I can confirm the stories have it all wrong.

First of all, no cemetery was ever placed anywhere because it looked like a good spot for serial killers or junkies. No priest inspected the land and thought, "Hey, this would be a great spot to scare everyone away from. I'll make sure my cemetery is dark and eerie, so all my parishioners will be frightened into walking the straight and narrow."

No, cemeteries are chosen with *peace* in mind. Peace for the dead, and for their mourners.

It helps a little with the grief to know your loved one will spend eternity with a view of the mountains, or the city they lived in, or the ocean. That they'll hear bird song and feel the sun on their face, watch the flowers bloom in spring.

Our cemetery is the most peaceful place in the village, to the point where many people will come here for their Sunday walk along the narrow paths between graves, or to do the last minute cramming for a test in the shade of the plane trees. Personally, I enjoy spring especially, when the wisteria are flowering all over the north wall and the sun hits just right as it rises behind the church spire before a single car has started up out in the civilized world of the living.

On days like today, I'll sometimes go all the way to the top of the church spire. I don't do it often, because I normally try to behave as closely to a living human being as possible—and this means not flying thirty meters off the ground—but the view from up there is just spectacular.

"It's going to rain in three days," I say with a smile. I'm holding onto the spire like I'm the hunchback of Notre Dame, one foot on the shingles, one in the air.

Clothilde, my ghostly friend of thirty years, is sitting on thin air next to me, her hands under her jeans-clad legs, her Converse-covered feet swinging back and forth. *She* has never bothered to follow the rules of the physical world.

"Really, Robert?" she teases me. "I didn't think you were *that* old."

Well, I'm a lot older than I look, but then so is she. We were respectively thirty-five and twenty when we died, so that's how we still look. But had we lived, I'd have been well into my sixties, and Clothilde somewhere in her early fifties.

Which is long enough to know the three day rule really works.

"When you can see the Pyrenees from Toulouse, it's going to rain in three days. That's the way it has always been, Clothilde, and you know it."

The entire mountain chain is visible today. From the Mediterranean in the east to the Atlantic in the west, these steep mountains separate France from Spain. In early spring, most of the highest peaks are still covered in snow, the deepest valleys dark shadows.

The mountains are supposedly the tomb of Pyrène, a beautiful woman who had an affair with Hercules after he'd finished the twelve labors. When Hercules decided he'd been away from home for too long, he left her, inadvertently exposing her to be killed by wolves. Learning she was dead, Hercules turned back and created this mountain chain in her honor, to represent how much they loved each other.

On days like this, the story feels true.

Join Robert and Clothilde as they escape their cemetery to investigate their own murders!

rwwallace.com

Of course, the funeral procession in progress below us might have influenced my opinion.

We were down there, on the church steps, when the door opened. That is usually when we'll discover if the deceased will be joining us as a ghost or not. Silence means no ghost; desperate and panicked screaming means new arrival. Today, there was nothing but silence.

From the casket.

But from the mourners, there was a *lot* of crying, pain and loss radiating off them in waves.

While we're used to seeing people working through their grief—cemeteries are more for the mourners than for the dead, after all—I just didn't want to absorb their sadness today.

The world is too beautiful not to be enjoyed—and maybe I'm too tired.

If the person didn't become a ghost, we don't need to listen in on the mourners, looking for clues. We can wait up here, admiring the Pyrenees as we chat.

Clothilde scowls at the mountains in the distance, challenging them to not bring us rain for once. Her mother was apparently a firm believer in this adage, and she'd like nothing more than to prove the old lady wrong.

I have no idea what the reason for this phenomenon is, why the air cleans up like that so we can see farther just before it rains, but I know it works. Not that I'll attempt to argue with Clothilde on the subject—I'll let the rain do the talking for me in three days.

We stay up on the roof until the last of the mourners leave. The priest's speech at the grave isn't much longer than usual, but it takes several hours for the cemetery to empty out. It seems like almost everyone wants to say a last, personal goodbye before leaving, and the people I believe to be the deceased's family wait until last, until everybody else has left, to have a collective breakdown as they look down on the casket waiting to be covered in dirt.

I'm glad we decided not to join the party—we've had our fair share of grief over the years, no need to add in extra.

Once we're the only ones left, we approach the fresh grave. Wanting to keep our distance from the mourners isn't the same as not wanting to pay our respects. We never let anyone get buried without at least a figurative tip of our hat.

"Isabelle Neumann," Clothilde reads off the temporary cross marking the spot until the gravestone can be installed. "Looks like you had a lot of people caring about you."

"Rest in peace," I add, thinking that is the last we'll hear of Isabelle.

Three days later, mere minutes after the rain comes pouring down from a bleak, gray sky, a head pops out of Isabelle's grave in complete silence. Long black hair, striking dark eyes, and a hoodie. I'd say she's somewhere in her early fifties.

I happen to be next to her grave when she crawls out of the ground, and if I'd still had a beating heart in my chest, I swear it would have stopped.

"You're a ghost," I say. Smooth for the guy who usually tries to ease the new arrivals into the realities of their new existence.

"Looks like it," she says as she climbs out of the ground, her voice oddly flat. She glances around the cemetery, spotting Clothilde sitting on her own gravestone some distance off and sparing an extra second or two for the church.

This is when everyone attempts to leave the cemetery—which we can't. Nobody has ever taken my word for it. The only thing that varies from ghost to ghost is the amount of time they'll spend trying to get past the gates anyway. Then through, over, or under the wall, and finally straight up to the sky. None of it works. We can't get past the wall or higher than the top of the church spire. I'm not sure where the limit is downward, but everyone who's tried has come back up eventually.

Isabelle doesn't try to leave, nor pester me with questions. She just releases a half-hearted sigh and sits down on the small mound marking her last resting place, before proceeding to study the raindrops falling through her outstretched hand.

"Ghost," she says.

———

I have a bit of a malfunction at first. Instead of talking to our new neighbor or letting her brood in peace, I just stand there, staring.

"You're going to catch flies," Clothilde says as she joins me five minutes later. "Did we miss her screams?"

"She didn't scream."

"Three days of *silence* to come to terms with being a ghost?" Clothilde whistles softly. "How is that even possible?"

Everybody scream when they wake up as a ghost in their casket. You're being buried alive, and the feeling of the casket being lowered into the ground, the sound of dirt hitting the lid… It freaks out the most hardened of veterans, and Clothilde and I were no exceptions. You're only let out of the casket once you come to terms with your new existence as a ghost.

Isabelle took as long as the rest of us if she only crawls out now—but not a single sound? No cry for help or mercy?

All right, time to take action. I step closer to Isabelle and go down on one knee so I can look her in the eye. "Hi. My name is Robert, and this is Clothilde. We're the only resident ghosts at the moment. You're Isabelle?"

Sighing, she tears her gaze away from her hand and looks at me. There's a flatness to her eyes that I don't like. "That's me," she says. "Nice to meet you."

"We, uh…" Without the usual barrage of questions, I'm not sure where to start. "We didn't think you'd become a ghost since we didn't hear you scream. Most people are quite scared when they wake up in their casket."

She glances at the dirt covering her final resting place. "Well, it wasn't fun. But when I yelled out, nobody reacted, so I figured it was soundproof or something." She shrugs. "Didn't seem like there was much point in wasting energy on screaming."

So she just decided to lie there, in her casket, and wait for death?

"I figured my energy would be better spent on trying to get out of there on my own, but nothing I did had the slightest impact on the casket, or on me." She holds up her hand again, watching the raindrops fall through it. "No scratch on the casket, no scratch on me. And the lack of hunger was a bit of a giveaway."

I'm glad Isabelle can't see the way Clothilde looks at her sideways.

"I was just going to lie down there forever," Isabelle continues. "But it got too boring, so I climbed up here. I don't suppose you have Netflix, to pass the time?"

I don't even know what that is. It's time to take control over the situation.

"As you can see," I say, waving a hand at the cemetery around us. "There aren't many ghosts here. That's because being a ghost isn't supposed to be permanent. Only people with unfinished business linger, and once they get their loose ends tied up, they move on. To what we suppose is a better place."

Still not much of a reaction from Isabelle. She's listening, but my words aren't having much of an impact. "Then why are you guys still here? You die recently, too?"

Ah, finally some familiar ground. This question is almost as frequent as "how do I leave?"

"We've been here for awhile and don't expect to be moving on anytime soon," I say as I get back up and step across the path to lean against the Sanchez tomb. I don't like having rain falling right through me because it's such a stark reminder that I no longer have a physical body, so in weather like this, I prefer hanging out near the larger graves that have roofs and overhangs like this one.

I offer Isabelle a sincere smile. "While we're waiting for our chance for closure, we've specialized in helping others find peace." I don't get into details. She doesn't need to know how we need to catch the people who killed us thirty years ago, worry about why Clothilde's headstone only has a first name and a date of death, or why I don't have more than a slight bump in the ground next to Clothilde to mark my final resting place.

Our time will come.

And in the meantime, I'm healing my guilty conscience by helping others.

Clothilde jumps onto the roof of the Sanchez grave, taking up her usual posture of sitting with her hands under her thighs, her feet swinging back and forth through the stone. "Do you know what you'll need to move on? I don't suppose you were murdered?"

Although I don't let it show, I feel increasingly guilty over skipping Isabelle's funeral. We thought she hadn't become a ghost and therefore stayed away, in order to protect ourselves from the grief of her mourners. Now, as a result, we don't know anything about the circumstances around her death or what her friends and family had to say.

Isabelle tips her head from side to side. "Depends on your definition of murdered, I suppose. I was run over by a bus on my way to work, but I hardly think the driver did it on purpose. I slipped on a patch of mud and just sort of slid onto the road."

Hit by a bus. Never had one of those before.

Isabelle laughs, and her eyes are suddenly more alive. "I wonder how many people at work made a joke about it." When she sees the shock on my face, her smile grows even bigger. "Relax, I don't mean that in a bad way. It's just one of those things that get discussed over and over. Everybody has to have a backup. What if the person responsible for a certain task suddenly gets sick, or hit by a bus? Will the project survive? Guess now they'll know."

While I'm not sure what to think, Clothilde loves the joke and laughs along with Isabelle. Since my friend died when she was only twenty years old, she has certain brooding teenager tendencies. I do my best to keep her happy, but it isn't always easy. So I appreciate it when someone manages to lift her spirits and takes her mind off her own fate.

"So I assume we can rule out murder," I say. "Is there any obvious unfinished business you think you need to take care of before moving on?"

Isabelle's smile disappears so completely I wonder if I imagined it. "Finishing my unfinished business from in here is going to be tricky."

"You'd be surprised at what we've managed so far." Yes, we're severely limited since we can't leave the cemetery and have but minimal influence on the living, but that hasn't stopped us in the past. After all, if Clothilde and I are the only ones left, it's because we've successfully helped everybody else.

Isabelle's lips lift, but the smile is flat, lifeless. "I can't leave the cemetery, right? Can't interact with people?"

I nod confirmation.

"What I need is to live my life. Feel like my life had meaning, that there was a point to it all. My life was just eat, work, sleep, an endless treadmill. And I was largely invisible to the people around me. The answer to the bus question when it comes to me was always 'it won't have an impact.'"

Her gaze roams our little cemetery, going over the gray and solemn tombs, the muddy paths, and the inaccessible outside world. "How do you propose I do that from in here?"

I'll probably never skip a funeral again. If we'd only listened in to the priest's speech when Isabelle was put in the ground, or her friends and family as they said their last goodbyes, we'd have had more ammunition, arguments.

There's no way someone with such a large funeral procession had no impact on the people around her. But no matter how I try to word it, Isabelle refutes my claims with a dismissive wave of her hand.

"They were there because they felt guilty about not caring. Why would they care? I never did anything worthwhile."

Clothilde, who usually lets me take care of discussions and arguments, shows no signs of leaving. She keeps moving closer to Isabelle, eyes never blinking, fascinated and annoyed with the other woman's refusal to recognize she was loved.

"You say you had two kids, right?" Clothilde asks. "That's 'doing something.' You gave life! You had a job, where you had enough responsibility for them to make sure you had a backup. That means something. And unless you have a really big family, there were a ton of friends at your funeral, which means you meant something to them." While the words are caring, Clothilde's tone is anything but. She's not the most patient person at the best of times, and when faced with someone she considers stupid, well…

Isabelle just sighs, completely oblivious to the teenaged ball of frustration spitting compliments at her. "In a week, they'll have forgotten I existed. My backup can do my job as well as I did, my kids still have their father and three aunts to look after them, and my friends never needed me to do anything."

Although she sometimes gets animated, Isabelle's eyes mostly stay flat and slightly unfocused. They remind me of a distant cousin, who spent his days watching TV or staring at the wall. My mother claimed he used to be the life of the party and full of energy, but a burnout at work sent him into a deep depression and he never made his way out.

What am I supposed to do with a depressed ghost?

Luckily, two days after Isabelle exiting her grave, two of her friends show up. I was sure it would happen sooner or later—how could it not, given the number of people at her funeral—but often, people wait until the gravestone is in place. I guess it feels cleaner, less visceral, than looking at the freshly dug dirt.

These clearly didn't want to wait. Two women in their early fifties, one with a long salt-and-pepper braid halfway down her back and the other with a short blonde pixie cut, slowly make their way from the parking lot, each with a potted plant in hand. They don't talk, but there's a definite feel of companionship.

"Flora and Geraldine," Isabelle says when I point out the visitors. "Friends from high school."

"You're still friends with people you went to school with?" I usher Isabelle along toward her grave so we'll be able to hear if the friends have anything to say. "That's impressive. Not everybody manages to maintain friendships for that long."

Isabelle shrugs. "None of us moved away. We had similar schedules. We were friends."

The two women arrive at Isabelle's grave and place their plants on either side of the temporary cross.

Isabelle eyes the flowers, and her shoulders lift slightly. They seem to have passed muster. But they're not proof her friends care.

Flora and Geraldine stay silent. If they're not going to talk of their own volition, I'm going to step in. We cannot afford to have them leave without showing Isabelle that her life wasn't meaningless.

"I bet you miss her," I say loudly. "Anything you would like to say to Isabelle while you're here?"

Isabelle rolls her eyes at me. And here I thought Clothilde was the only one of us who'd use that mode of communication.

"Sometimes they need a nudge," I explain. "Just standing there staring at your grave isn't going to give us any answers. While they can't hear our exact words, most people at least get... the general gist of the emotion or idea we're trying to convey."

That catches her interest. Isabelle walks up to the short-haired woman—Flora—and bends forward to look her friend in the eye. "You don't need come here, Flora," she says kindly. "No need to feel guilty. Just get on with your life."

Clothilde rushes forward to place herself between Isabelle and her friend. "What do you think you're doing?"

Isabelle stares daggers at Clothilde. "Helping my friend, what does it look like I'm doing? There's no need for her to feel sad or guilty. Just because my life is over doesn't mean hers has to be."

Clothilde throws her hands in the air but holds her ground, denying Isabelle direct contact with her friend.

"I bet you *don't* feel guilty," I say, making sure both Flora and Geraldine can hear me. "I bet you're here because you miss your friend and you want to remember her and pay your respects."

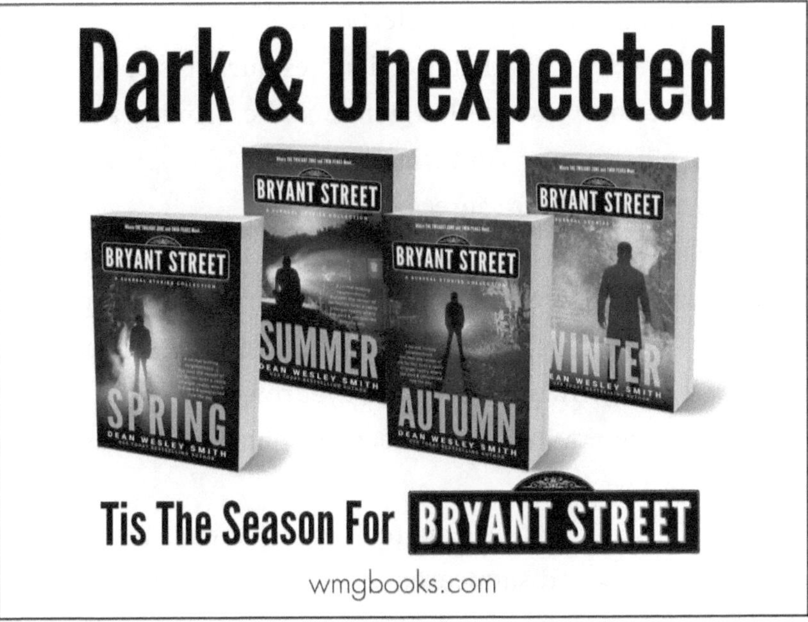

Isabelle throws me another murderous glance as she stomps over to Geraldine, Clothilde in tow. "Just go—"

"I really miss her," Geraldine says so softly I can barely hear her.

Flora, who doesn't have the interference of two shouting ghosts, catches the words just fine. "Me too. How are we supposed to go to restaurants, or plays, or silly touristy boat rides without her?"

"You just go, that's how!" Isabelle has stopped smack on top of the mound marking her grave, unable to decide which friend she should yell at first.

But it's not all anger. None of it, probably. She seems genuinely worried her friends will lose sleep over her absence or stop having fun without her. Weirdly enough, it comes from a position of love.

"People need time to mourn, Isabelle," I say softly. "It's not fun, but an important part of life. Of love."

"We should go to that Belgian restaurant she loved so much," Geraldine says with a gentle smile. "And get mussels and fries in her honor. And wine."

"Lots of wine," Flora agrees.

Isabelle doesn't seem to have anything to say to that. When her friends continue reminiscing, remembering all of Isabelle's favorite activities and spots, she quiets down and listens, a slight frown between her eyebrows.

"Seems like you had an impact on their lives," I say when her friends have left.

Isabelle stays at the cemetery gate, staring at the spot where their car disappeared between two houses. She stopped telling her friends to move on with their lives like she'd never existed, but instead of her feeling better about herself, she seems to be slipping back into apathetic mode.

"You always think you have more time, you know?" She's mostly talking to herself, but I nod in agreement.

If I'd known my last days on earth were just that, there are a lot of things I'd have done differently. People I'd have told how much they meant to me, new things I'd have tried. Mistakes I'd have unmade.

If what Isabelle needs is acceptance that this is it, anything she put off for later will stay undone, then I'm not sure how to help her.

I haven't figured out how to come to grips with that myself.

———

Isabelle's gravestone becomes something of a fixation for her once it's installed. Her name gleams brightly in gold whenever a ray of sunlight pierces the gray clouds, leaving a black empty spot below it for whenever her husband will join her. She's been staring at that smooth surface for days, her worry lines deepening.

I haven't bothered walking over to talk to her about it because I suspect she doesn't expect her husband to *want* to be buried with her. Unless he has an untimely accident like her, he won't be along for several decades, which would give him plenty of time to find someone else, remarry, want to be buried with the new and better wife. Then Isabelle will be stuck here for all eternity with the empty patch on the headstone as a reminder that she's well and truly alone and worthless.

It's all too easy to know what's going on in that gloomy head of hers. I've tried convincing her that her life had meaning, taking any approach I can think of. She waves it all off with a huff. Clothilde has done the same—and I just wish Isabelle knew my friend well enough to realize what it takes to get Clothilde to give people compliments—to no avail.

Isabelle's unfinished business is living a life that has meaning, and there's no way to do that from here.

So the only line of attack open to me is convincing her the life she led *did* have meaning. No amount of explaining or argumentation from Clothilde or me is going to make a difference, of course, but the words of her friends and family might.

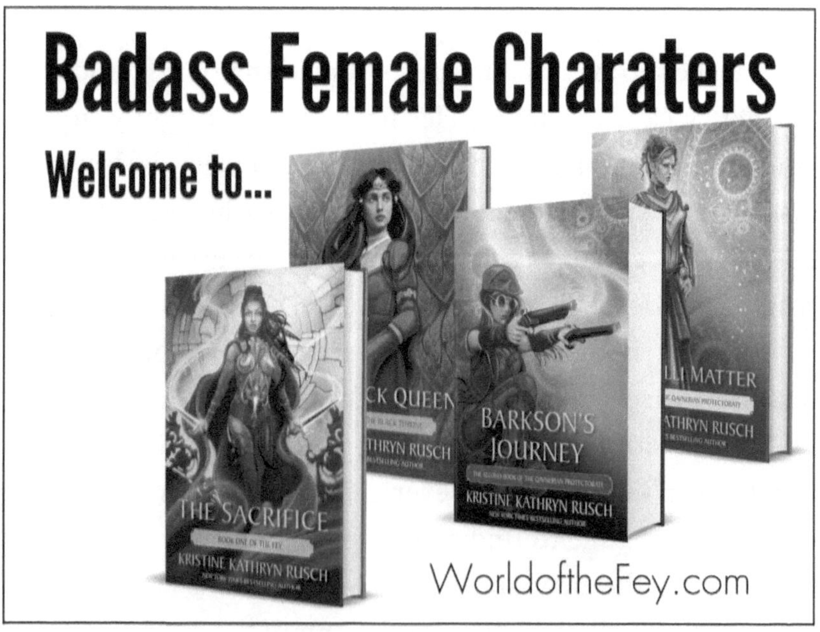

Her kids, who show up the day after the gravestone is installed, should be the ideal candidates.

They're two boys, aged fifteen and seventeen. One is tall and lanky with curly hair and doesn't look the least bit like his mother, while the other is a carbon copy of Isabelle, except younger and male. They're both dragging their feet as they cross the cemetery, pushing their bikes next to them down the gravel path. They don't talk, just advance slowly in gloomy silence, their eyes on the ground.

"I'm glad you came to visit your mother," I say as I fall into step with them. "She's been feeling a bit down and could use a morale boost."

Not everyone is sensitive to ghosts. I don't know what trait or characteristic make some people take in what we say to them on a subconscious level and others go on with their lives as if we were never there, I just know that every attempt at intervention is something of a hit and miss. Isabelle's friends seemed to hear us well enough, but kids are often completely immune.

Maybe they're too innocent. Unaware of the fate awaiting us all in the end.

The tall boy lifts his eyes to glance around the cemetery. "You think Maman is happy with being here? This place doesn't have much of a view."

Ah, I think he may have heard me.

"She didn't exactly go out of her way to find beautiful views when she was alive," the younger boy replies sullenly. "Seemed happy to just stare at the wallpaper all day."

"She was sick." The young man's voice is firm. He has no doubts about this.

Looks like it wasn't the dying that made Isabelle depressed. I can't tell if that's a good thing or not.

We're getting close to Isabelle's grave, where she's waiting for her sons, standing next to her headstone with her hands clasped in front of her. The usual dullness in her eyes is absent, but unfortunately, nothing soft or loving has taken its place.

She's going to try to kick her sons out of here the same way she attempted with her friends.

"You try to tell them not to mourn you or push them to leave before they're ready and I'm sending Clothilde after you." I keep my voice low so the boys won't be confused if they catch onto my curt tone. "Clothilde has haunted this cemetery for thirty years. Believe me when I say you do *not* want her coming for your sanity."

Isabelle's eyes flash. "You can't tell me how to talk to my own boys."

"And I won't. As long as you don't do anything that will be detrimental to them. Not allowing them to grieve their mother falls under that category."

Isabelle doesn't reply, but the way she juts out her jaw tells me that is exactly what she wanted to do.

The boys lean their bikes against the tomb on the other side of the path and come to stand awkwardly at the foot of their mother's grave.

"Now what?" the young one asks.

"Now you tell your mother how much she meant to you," I tell them. "Imagine she's here, hearing everything you say."

Isabelle rolls her eyes and I'm *this* close to calling Clothilde.

The eldest of the boys proves his sensitivities for ghosts. "We talk to her. Anything you need to get off your chest, now's your chance."

"You think she's listening?" The brother sneers, but it's at least partly bravado to cover up the emotions he's bound to be feeling underneath. "That she's an angel looking down on us from heaven? As if."

I'm about to confirm that yes, their mother is listening, but the elder brother doesn't need it.

"Doesn't hurt to try, does it? What if she *is* here? Do you think she'd be happy to hear you pretend not to care? And if she isn't, well… It's not exactly going to hurt us."

Some of Isabelle's cold front melts as she watches her sons battle their grief. I hope she can see this conversation isn't only needed for her, but also for her kids. Losing their mother as such a young age would be difficult even if she *was* a terrible mother—which I'm fully convinced she wasn't.

"I hope you like the headstone," the eldest says, staring at his mother's name carved into the granite. "I helped Papa pick it out. He couldn't figure out which one you'd like best."

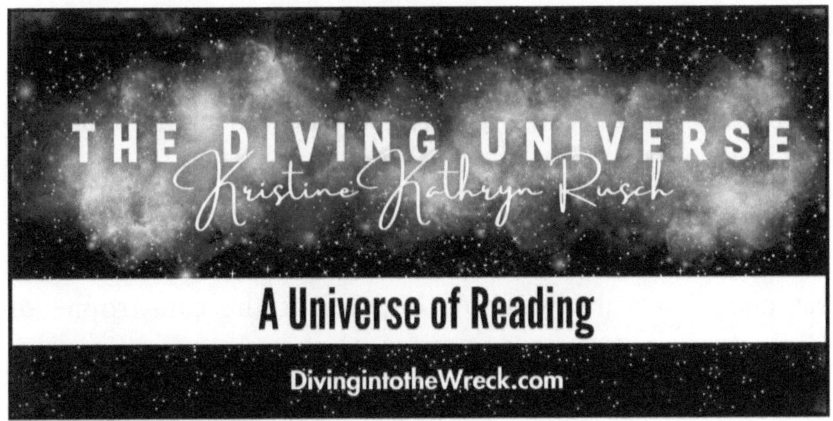

Frown deepening, Isabelle takes a step toward her son. After a quick, annoyed look in my direction, she places a hand on her son's shoulder. "It's lovely, *chéri*. You chose well."

The boy nods once. "I think you'd have liked it."

"Papa doesn't know how to function without you." It seems the youngest has decided to join in after all. "This morning, he spent two hours staring at your stuff in the closet, only to leave everything in place and closing the door."

Isabelle is in front of her son in an instant. "He just needs some time, *chéri*. He'll throw out my stuff when he's ready."

I wince but figure the boy will get the sentiment she's trying to convey and not the actual words.

"I don't want him to get rid of your stuff," the boy whispers. "What if I forget you?"

Isabelle opens her mouth to answer, but I beat her to it. "If you're going to tell him to forget you as soon as he can, I swear to God…"

She shuts up, proving me right. This woman is unbelievable.

All right, my priority is no longer Isabelle. She's going to have to figure out her stuff in due time, but a mourning fifteen-year-old takes precedence. "You won't forget your mother," I tell him. "Even if you should have no physical reminders of her, you'll always remember her and what she meant to you."

The older brother picks up on my message. "Don't worry, Mathias, we'll remember her. You think you'll ever be able to eat chocolate cake without thinking of the catastrophe of your eighth birthday?"

Mathias barks a laugh, apparently surprising himself.

Isabelle groans, her shoulders slumping.

"Twelve kids spitting chocolate cake all over the living room, behaving like they're going to die of poisoning because Maman got the salt and sugar mixed up? I've never been able to trust any kind of brown cake since."

The boys keep reminiscing about the cake incident, their smiles widening, bodies animatedly reenacting their friends' reactions. If anybody saw them without knowing the context, they'd be shocked someone would behave like this in a cemetery. I think it's wonderful.

But none of it makes Isabelle smile. She looks heartbroken and shattered.

I step away from the boys so we won't interfere with their joyful reliving of a favorite memory of their mother. "Isabelle, do you not see that this is a *good* memory for them?"

"Remembering how big of a failure I was as a mother? Sure, great. You really think this is going to convince me they're not better off without me?"

"I really do. Look at them, Isabelle. Look at their expressions, listen to their words. There's no mocking, no criticism. They're not bemoaning how you made all their friends spit out their food. They're remembering a moment in their lives they found hilarious, something they'll remember forever. Something they associate with you.

"It's not uncommon for us to love people as much for their mistakes as for their successes. For example, my grandfather never learned how to drive, so my grandmother was the one to drive them everywhere. Whenever someone commented, he grumbled something about his leg not feeling right so he couldn't take the wheel. It's that grumpy old idiot that I remember, and with much fondness."

It's going to take more than one silly anecdote to convince Isabelle, but she doesn't look quite as miserable as a minute ago. She even manages a smile when her youngest rolls around on the ground, imitating one of his friends who was convinced he was going to die.

The boys don't need any more prompting from us to keep reminiscing. They bring up a couple of more anecdotes of Isabelle messing up in a way they found hilarious, before moving on to softer moments, where she helped them save a bird who'd fallen out of its nest or patched them up after they fell out of a tree or crashed their bikes.

I keep Isabelle company as she observes them, never saying a word. She's mostly enjoying being around her boys, listening to them laugh, but I think she's also seeing some of what I've been trying to tell her—that her life did mean something.

When the boys leave, their steps lighter, she's still here, though. It wasn't enough for her to move on.

We settle in to wait for whoever her next visitor might be, hoping they'll be the one to help her see her own worth.

———

It took him long enough to work up the courage to come here, but Isabelle's husband shows up ten days later. Since I didn't participate in the funeral, I don't know how he normally looks, but I bet those dark circles under his eyes are a new addition. The utterly desolated slump to his shoulders, too.

I've been making *some* leeway with Isabelle. She has admitted her children were better off with her than without her and that she had a meaningful influence on them—and not just for creating them in the first place.

But it's not enough for her to move on.

I think she needs to have existed for something other than her children. It's not a situation I can identify with, having died childless, but I guess it makes a certain amount of sense if she has spent the last seventeen years putting her sons ahead of her own needs.

She expected to get time to live her own life later, once they were out of the house, but now it's too late. And what she did have the time for just isn't enough, apparently.

The husband has brought flowers. A dozen red roses, not something we see too often in our cemetery. They're popular for Valentine's in the outside world, but they just don't set the right mood around here.

"I know how you love roses," the husband whispers as he places the bouquet on Isabelle's grave. "The florist recommended I get you something else, but I'd rather get you something inappropriate you like than something seemly that you hate."

"That's sweet of him," Clothilde comments. She's perching on Isabelle's headstone, her feet swinging back and forth through the granite. She hasn't even tried to help me in my argumentation with Isabelle these past weeks, but she isn't about to miss out on meeting the husband.

He's kind of our last hope. If he can't convince his wife her life had meaning, nobody can. Then Isabelle will be stuck with us here forever.

We're all mostly ignoring the slight drizzle that has kept the whole place gloomy for the past five days, although Clothilde frequently sends me dirty looks as if it's my fault for giving voice to the three-day rule the day of Isabelle's funeral. Isabelle's husband is wearing a raincoat, but he hasn't bothered to pull up the hood. I suspect he doesn't even realize his hair is soaked.

"Thank you for the flowers," Isabelle says, a slight smile playing on her lips. "They're lovely."

Looks like the husband made the right choice.

I consider prodding him to talk to his wife, to tell her how much she meant to him, but I decide to wait. I'll see what he does on his own, and whether or not Isabelle chooses to pull anything out of him. If they don't figure something out by themselves, I'll step in.

"I miss you," the husband whispers to Isabelle's name on the headstone.

I expect him to go into the usual spiel of how he can't believe she's gone, how lost he'll be without her. I figure that if Isabelle hears it enough, she'll end up accepting to move on.

But the husband takes a different tack. "I wanted to thank you, Isabelle," he says, "for the life we had together. Who knows where I would have ended up without you. Probably not happy. And certainly not with two wonderful sons."

Although she knows the man infinitely better than us, Isabelle also seems surprised by his words. She was ready to interject and contradict, ready to argue for her husband to forget all about her and move on with his life, but now her mouth slams shut. Her eyes blink, repeatedly, as if she's having trouble making sense of what her husband is saying.

The husband keeps talking. "You helped me mature, figure out what I wanted in life. You showed me it was possible to have fun, even as a 'serious adult.'" He and Isabelle both smile as he makes air quotes—it must be some sort of inside joke between them.

"What I wanted was you." The husband kicks the tip of his shoe into Isabelle's grave. Not aggressive in any way, more of a nudge. Something that would have been sweet if he could have bumped into Isabelle's leg instead of her tombstone.

"And now I have to figure out the rest of it alone."

Isabelle puts a hand on her husband's forearm. At first, her hand goes right through, but she is a quick study and figures out how to convince her own hand it is as solid as the arm it's touching. "You'll do fine, Vincent. The boys will help you."

Vincent huffs. "The boys are already starting to step up by pushing me to come here today. They not-so-gently suggested this would do me more good than staring at your clothes, pretending I'm anywhere near ready to get rid of them. Letting go of you."

Clothilde and I exchange a glance. This is promising, right?

Once it's clear Isabelle isn't going to pull one of her stunts, we leave them to it. We stay close enough to get the gist of what they're saying to each other, but far enough that we can all pretend we don't.

I can tell the moment Isabelle starts envisioning the possibility that her life did have some sort of impact on the world through her husband. Her words to Vincent change, from trying to get him to forget her to getting more details, more proof. Making sure it's all true.

I think she forgets he can't actually hear her. He's obviously sensitive to ghosts, so his subconscious is getting the messages, but no living being has ever heard our actual words. Yet Isabelle keeps talking to him, asking questions, as if they were having a conversation.

And Vincent delivers. Isabelle *has* been an important influence on his life. He really wouldn't have been the same if they'd never met. And he's happy about the man she helped him become.

When he leaves the cemetery, Isabelle is already fading.

"I told you your life had meaning," I tell her gently as I come up next to her. "And although your friends and family will miss you, they were all better off having known you."

"Looks like you're right," Isabelle says with half a smile. "Now I just wish I'd realized it sooner."

I shrug. "Better late than never."

Clothilde comes over to say goodbye before Isabelle disappears completely, then it's just the two of us again. Waiting our turn to solve *our* unfinished business.

Until that day comes, we'll help other ghosts move on, gaze at the view of the Pyrenees from the church spire on clear days, and admire the birds and flowers in spring. We'll even figure out how to enjoy rainy days like today, and fight away any hint of gloom.

I could think of worse ways to spend my days.

MIKE ZIMMERMAN

Mike Zimmerman returns for a third appearance in these pages after his fun "AB" story in Issue Thirty. Mike clearly knows his beers, and a few of my friends (looking at you Kevin J. Anderson and Mark Leslie) will just flat love this story. And more than likely understand it a ton more than I do.

Mike is a full-time bestselling writer, editor, and brand storyteller who specializes in finding and honing a person/place/product's unique voice. He has done that across a multitude of divergent brands — from publicly-traded companies to national magazines to B2B mavens to household-name authors.

He uses journalism, research, analytics, good prose chops, razor-sharp copywriting, a bent brain, and a sense of humor to create world-class content for any audience. With far over 50 books in print, including 35 novels, you can find out more about Mike at zimwrites.com including information about his new book Jet Lag Is For Suckers.

HOPHEAD

MIKE ZIMMERMAN

Naming is one of the great pleasures in life.

You get to name your kids, that's probably the biggest one. Should a wife change her name for her new husband? Or later on, to escape him? Entire cities evacuate bowels debating team names. Entrepreneurs wallow in their mission to capture the perfect word for their unicorn, entertainment production companies wink at the audience from their vanity cards, and food cartels spend millions getting you to fatten yourself on their latest name for chocolate and emulsifiers.

But who shoulders the greatest creative naming responsibility of all? Stakes hardly matter, which is why certain men would argue it's the fantasy sports enthusiast, naming their baseball teams after Ohtani's bookie or their Great Dane's lone testicle. Others would say it's the aspiring rock band, the Caca-Roaches, the Jack Talk Thais, and the Stinky Pinkies of your local bar scene.

No. The naming of all naming resides with the American craft beer brewer.

Marty Skenes fancied herself the best brewer in the world (undiscovered) and so knew she must have the greatest beer names in the world for her creations. She made her beers in rural eastern Pennsylvania from bespoke softened well water and competed with some of the best-named beers just in her time zone, the Eviscerated Pathway of Beauties and the Prison City Mass Riots and the Focal Bangers and good God did the lazy cliches and bad puns still sell and sell? Hopsolutely.

But now Marty, named just that, not short for anything, after a grandfather she never knew, had a new brew.

The greatest brew she'd ever tasted.

The brew that would change everything. Especially the world.

What to name it?

What the fuck to name it.

The men in her orbit formed an endless line, a queue of crave. Red-eyed and dark-bearded and basketball-bellied, nice guys full of a niceness slowly diluted by alcohol, any offenses offset by excellent tipping, a truth they believed of themselves: I'm a good guy. And she was what they wanted, a physical beauty providing gorgeously crafted and packaged and marketed nectar, her taps as teats and them like rakish knights at a daily banquet table toasting life and life and life once again and betcha she fucks like a sailor do you think she'd fuck me? I'm a good guy.

And there's that one guy. The obvious guy. The nicest most definitely goodest guy who also drank the most and fell into vats of foamy flattery while fawning over her simultaneous juiciness and dankness, multiple truths can hold and that's what makes the brew (her) so perfect. While all the while within his whispered words was him wailing look at my lust *oops it's dripping sorry do you have a bar towel.*

A man with a thousand-beer stare. Each night a ten-beer leer.

Yes. That guy.

The Nesbitt hop was the key to it all. But it was torture enough naming the hop after the man who bred it. Marty could never use the word Nesbitt to name a beer.

And oh the beer.

Not just a new flagship brew. A defining substance, a foundational aberration, a hall of fame guarantee, a thing all will imitate and fail to duplicate.

Because none can. None of them have what Marty has.

The Nesbitt hop.

Marty named her brewpub Anthracite Brewing Company, straightforward and necessary for the region's positive response, naming it after the county while also harking back to an early 20th century brewery of the same name. A solid name. She served four core brews, the hard pilsner, Easy, the wheaty Leaving Nutbush, the stout Chocolate Monk, and the original flagship IPA, Are You Obsequious? She brewed interstitials and seasonals as well, all the cutesy brews that kept them lining up for new cannings. Her place was a three thousand square-foot industrial space in Uther, Pennsylvania tucked away from the downtown not far from Uther College. An old shoe factory that could still produce whiffs of leather in far corners. But the brewkettle smells now ruled all.

A bar. Hightop tables. Eight taps. No kitchen, rotating food trucks out back in the grotto.

And the grotto.

Marty bought the majority of her hops, the Simcoe, the Nelson-Sauvin, the Citra, the Chinook, the Cascade, the Columbus, the Centennial, she brewed a DIPA just from the C-word hops called The C Word. But she wanted to grow her own. Pennsylvania was not perfect hop growing country, but good enough. She bordered the outdoor grotto seating space with low planters and kept the soil pH at 6.8, girl plants and boy plants alternating boy girl boy, and a-climbing they went. Hops grow upwards, real climbers, and require cross-pollinating, and these plants were all still young, three to six years old, beautiful creepers that eventually covered the grotto in aromatic greenery and turned the sunshine emerald on the best Sundays.

Marty was a flower girl, and the only flower she cared about was the hop. The little cone full of glands and flavor and aroma and bitterness and fruitiness and piney perfection popping with little explosions of lupulin as idiosyncratic as any grape or broadleaf tobacco or intercontinental coffee bean.

And at the back of the grotto, lording over them all, the only plant that mattered. The Nesbitt. A male hop plant, a freak, climbing up like all the others but also outward from a thick green trunk in an extra-deep dirt bed. A fifteen-foot wingspan easily. The flower pods slightly larger than normal hops and redder, like little alcoholic noses.

No one much commented on the Nesbitt side of the grotto. Marty fielded all manner of hop questions. But she never said the word Nesbitt, never gave away her secret nor her secret ingredient.

She hated its presence and could not live without it.

———

The ten-beer leer always devolved into the gusher of compliments. He soaked his feet in her lake of ale while staring at her and praising her skill. Her pours. Her creativity. Her mastery. Her dedication. Her patience. Her magic. Where did it all come from, he'd mumble, what was it (she) all about. Each kind word or phrase an obvious arm over her shoulder while the other hand wished away buttons and fabric and undergarments from across the bar. And then one night she glimpsed something, or did she, a dusty greenscale in his flesh, in his frownlines, caked in his arm hair. And later one night, grayish green flakes hanging off him. How could that be. She watched the beer drain from his glass faster than she could refill it. And perhaps knew the answer.

That night she invited him into the off-limits area.

He told her what he wanted. Of course he did.

Then she took him into the old factory basement. Of course she did.

She promised him all her beer. More than he could ever drink in a lifetime. And not just that. He would be the first. Always the first.

He accepted her terms, like all men, not understanding them.

———

All great businesses serve an addiction.

Marty admired the chemical arts. How can one not marvel at the signature synthetics of Pop-Tarts, of Doritos, of Oreos. God such perfection. Unmatched in their engineered abuse potential except by heroin and tobacco. But when crafting a highly-addictive substance out of only a handful of natural ingredients and not two dozen lab-engineered chemicals, those ingredients must become more muscular and carry far more weight than all the other products out there like it. Because in this business, if you make it right, if you make it cool, they stand in line for you, they must have you, their deprivation curiosity of some new mystery canning seethes in their brains. And thus we see how American food culture has escalated in the past forty years, rivaling and surpassing superior foreign wine, coffee, cheese, chocolate, bread, liquor, gastronomy, and yes, beer. And with the need for further muscularity of ingredients, so come more assertive hop flavors, higher alcohol, richer fruit and cocoa infusions, and when all else fails, bigger fucking cans.

Thinking those thoughts got Marty high.

That's what I do. That is my art. Ownership of them all.

And they jostled at her bar, surrounded the hightops, lined the walls, the grotto, the sidewalk around the block on release days, the hipster alcoholics deep in the throes of self-defined … hobbyism, rationalizations so thick you could club someone to death with them. All kinds: Cyclists on long rides, ex-jocks entertaining clients, card players, sports junkies, lost husbands, lost fathers, lost souls. They spent their time guzzling disguised as sipping while misunderstanding and discussing brewing chemistry and lupulin varietals and mango puree and Marty, that Marty, lookit her, her hair's up today, oh that beergirl genius without a boyfriend. Why not me?

The culture was such a boy thing. At first. Boys inevitably came in with their girls. Always tolerating the brewpub, the girls.

But now some of the girls drank too.

Cross-pollination.

The only way you get good flowers.

Fill their growlers, their glasses, their souls, one and all.

———

H*e tasted everything she made. As promised, he was first. Living down there and in the back and in the ground, eyes set, nose sniffing for the pour, the foam, lips quaking, sampling, then siphoning. Smiling when he liked a beer. And this went on and she wondered what would happen and soon it happened. His hair grew, his beard thickened, belly fattened but she also noticed his flakes, his scales, his leafy skin sporting fibrous veins and his odor and he craved more asked for more bring it bring it you are beauty incarnate for this, and he kept growing and spoiled and became horrid.*

She tied him to a trellis in the basement. She slid his bare deformed feet into soil she kept at a precise pH of 6.8.

———

D on't park in the pizzeria lot next door. Use the street. Aside from that, her customers did exactly what they should do and Marty printed money.

Now what she needed were names. Lotsa lotsa genius names. Line them up the way auto manufacturers stockpiled words like trailblazer and lumina and ophis.

Names for beers. Go:

Bugsy Seagull. Nah, too cutesy. Sounds like something brewed in Wildwood.

The Flies Shall Feast. Maybe for a Halloween ale.

Shinebox. Hey that might play.

Cause of Death. Google it, probably already taken, and stupid. Guys want to feel clever and ironic and elevated for drinking a beer.

Zigzag Ziptie. Just goofy enough for a session IPA.

Ligature Marks. Oh stop it.

Toebeans. Maybe a charity brew for a pet rescue.

Gorilla Salad. Yes. Save that one.

Acannaday. Doofuses might just get it.

The Tingler. Hmmm.

It's hard, It's really really hard. Those fuckers at Tired Hands are so good at this.

Manpain.

Wait. Say that again.

Manpain.

Yes, Manpain. That was the one. The one name for this one beer. In big goddamn letters on a big goddamn can.

———

At night she bathed him in artificial sun, no windows, and harvested from him. She plucked his flowers. Always taking the first one and rubbing it to wet crumbly smears in her palms and breathing it into her soul. Something ungodly, no other hop aroma like it. But there was more. She put her hands in his soil. Smelled the compost. Pushed deeper. Feeling his toes and roots squirming through soil. Wet, sticky roots, like fingers no one ever licked clean. Once even his proximity disgusted her. The man clearly an eater, an ejaculator, a farter. Now his touch was as welcome as her own hands while bathing herself, a lover's touch when it's just getting to know everything about her. And then she saw a strange stem hanging off him, a new growth. Something wet there. A bubble drop hanging off its tip. She dabbed a pinky. Smelled it. Felt an awak-

ening in her nose and palate. Oh my... She touched her pinky to her tongue.

Holy god. Holy god.

Marty took the sample to her brewlab and began plans.

And then she returned and milked him and milked him and milked him and his whole being shook and she could barely prevent herself from guzzling the sap.

———

Marty held a private launch party for the new beer. She invited the die hards, the regulars, some local press, hipster influencers, the college paper, a radio station. Of a hundred people she was one of three women in attendance. She thought of making the Nesbitt hop part of the info dump she made about the brew, but decided no, say nothing.

Marty cleaned up okay when she wanted to, ha ha. Her smile could disarm, and tonight her smile was genuine.

And the beer poured.

And they quivered. They didn't even talk. They just drank and quivered.

Such a glorious combination of creaminess and juiciness and bitterness and … something else. It seemed so simple and yet perfectly elusive. "What is it? What is this?"

It's a secret.

And Marty basked as they all said it or thought it or wished it as their motherserver fetishes bull-charged through their brains incapacitating all else.

Eyes following her everywhere.

Each one of them waiting their turn to be next to her. To happen for her. The Bellinger hop … the Fekete hop … the Ashton hop. Ashton was married, he should look at her like he looks at my beer.

I can have them all.

I can *name* them all.

———

I t's hard to know what an unusual ingredient will do to a brew, but somehow Marty knew. He grew under the heat lamps and became swampier, nonverbal, fluttering, shaking limbs and stems and flaunting his flowers. She kept feeding him beer and checking his pH. He was no longer recognizable and his periodic ripenings no longer had anything to do with seasons or sunshine. She squeezed him dry until it was time to squeeze him again. It all went into the kettles. And Marty noticed more. Herself. Green flaky dust coming off her, probably exhaust from his leavings. Maybe. And such a pleasant whiff...

———

Manpain was a freight train.

Limited batches meant the line on canning days was a quarter-mile long.

Marty was talked about in the online beer press and in places she never even heard about, the brew queen, the beer princess, the hop hottie, the lupulin lovely. Yes, someone called her the lupulin lovely, it's on TikTok.

She let them talk. She remained silent. She smiled at her customers. She tapped their beers. She poured 'em perfect. She sold plenty of her old beers and still made fun new beers … she did Gorilla Salad as a saison … but everyone wanted the Manpain.

She maxed out her hours against what she could earn without outsourcing her production. A business ceiling. She eyed another factory in town for expansion, the new place, three stories, an old cage elevator, kitsch on kitsch on kitsch printing money.

Marty, by normal American culture standards, had reached the point of true wealth and stature, a ledger full of priceless IP, kettles full of joy, customers drooling on her bartop, all of it different shades of liquid gold.

———

And finally she was no longer afraid of what people might see and she transplanted him from the basement to the grotto. No small operation, but she had time and will. And he would be just another climbing hop in a small jungle of them. But this one flour-

ishing and 10 feet tall now, spreading wide, with a soft pulpy trunk and, hidden by leaves, the parts she milked after hours. Sometimes she heard people wonder when Jimmy Nesbitt left town and where the fuck he wound up.

———

Business out of control. Must brew more.

Dudes grinning, drinking, urging her, faces hovering over her in the dark, come on, do it do it yes more more more.

They're all fatter now, bellies hard as barrels, piss smelling like pine cones.

Food trucks stop coming — all they want is the beer.

You are my hero, one says, a goddess, lookit you. Lookit you.

Have another drink, kiddo, she says.

Yes another, he says. I love a woman who talks sense.

———

Late night. Humid and silent in the grotto.

She climbs him, naked.

It works, more and more sap.

She never knew it could be so good, not with anyone, not Nesbitt, but oh God yes Nesbitt.

She is the flower now.

What comes out of him goes into the kettles.

And for the first time, what comes out of her goes in there too.

———

Out in the grotto, on sunny weekends, the really perfect days for drinking in the sun, the hop plants quiver when she's near and people notice and edge away.

She brews naked because clothes hurt.

Tasting.

Always tasting now.

All good businesses serve an addiction.

All good things.

All good *things* serve an addiction.

———

Beer dudes file in. They drink and drink. Line out the door. Taps open at all times filling growlers and crowlers and pints and flights. Change kegs. Pour more. Print that money.

How come nobody gets with you, one asks. Not even girls. Who are you?

She smiles. Slips her two fingers into the guy's beer, pulls them out and slips them into her own mouth.

Holy shit, he says.

———

Marty can hold it off no longer. It happens on a sunbright Saturday the first week of college football, the bar packed, fresh batch of Manpain on tap, new TVs everywhere for all the games and about a quarter past two she staggers from some place down below and bounces off people and tables and there's spillage and at least one broken glass and she is completely naked, not even a hair tie or little earring in sight.

To say silence falls is an old chestnut as old as chestnuts, but one could hear this particular silence fall across them like a wave following her nude form from the bar out to the grotto. More than one man thanks God for the sight.

Outside, the people part and the hop plants sing and shake.

Whispers and expletives and pointed fingers follow her, phones record her and not one person says stop it.

She is done tolerating and smiling and producing for them.

She pushes past one last table knocking over pints, simultaneously stepping up and falling into the forest of Nesbitt.

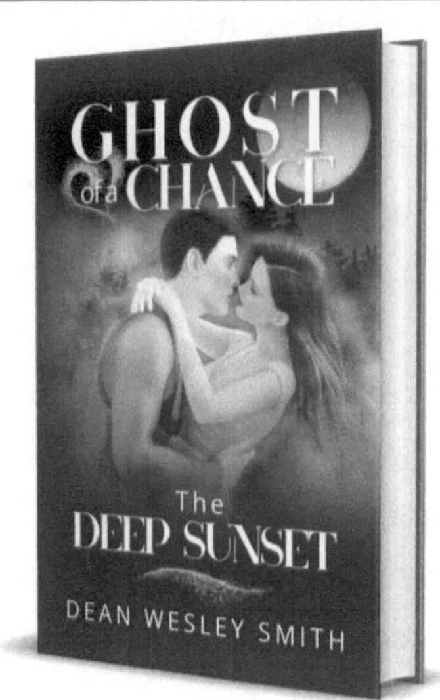

Marty cries out and no one can tell if it's pain or pleasure or destiny and when a couple of noble men step forward to rescue her from whatever this is, she wails again and it's rage and she turns back to level her stare and they stop and some of Nesbitt envelopes her and tears into her and enters her flesh and that's when the people fall into a backwards retreat and then a run.

Marty backs herself into Nesbitt harder now, her form jerking with the force of green reedy limbs piercing her skin and slipping under it as she merges with the front of the massive plant's torso.

And what really sends them flying, the Nesbitt thing whipping into some kind of spasm or frenzy or ritual and it moans and moans in the deepest kind of agony release.

That's when its giant stem rips loose from its earth and it sways to keep itself upright, tearing itself from the climbing trellis and wires strung to aid its spread.

The hop plant urges itself forward, loose now, its thick stem doing its best to mimic the waddle of actual feet but it can only be a single trunk dragging wet drooling roots.

It lets off another wail from something resembling a mouth. It sounds like a low rageful loooooookkaaaaaat-meeeeeee.

The people explode for the exits on that. They grab their beers as they fly, chugging to finish, picking up growlers and tucking them like footballs, looting the coolers behind the bars for four-packs, all as the thing moves forward into the bar proper, displaying a rictus-faced Marty as its chest emblazon.

Not everyone runs.

A few, the unsurprising few if one spent any time at all at the brewery, keep their seats at the bar and continue to drink Manpain.

"Lookit this fucked up shit," Fekete says, glass in hand.

"I am … Hophead!" it bellows, surveying them.

"Here's to you, dude," Bellinger says, raising his glass in tribute, because it was all in the naming of the thing.

"That Marty in there?" Fekete asks, leaning forward to see. "No shit. It is. Huh."

"Fuck this, I'm pouring my own," says Ashton and he bellyflops over the bar and opens a tap for himself.

"Hophead will rule!" Hophead bellows, waddling closer to the bar.

Ashton turns back to his barmates and gestures at Hophead as he sips and says, "You know, last night some dude went through something similar at that restaurant in the remodeled railroad station, that gastro place that almost shut down."

"Melt?" Fekete asks.

"That's the one," Ashton replies.

Hophead listens intently. "What is it you say."

Ashton shrugs at Hophead. "I didn't see, I just heard. Some fuckin foodie wound up in your situation. Doesn't look like you, looks different, they said he was bibb lettuce in the garage or something but same shit, I guess. He busted out. Calls himself Mouthfeel."

Hophead ponders that. "Mouthfeel … a name for sure."

"Fucked up," Bellinger says.

"S'what I heard, fuck do I know," Ashton says.

And then they hear a tiny, reedy sound. A shredded voice

saying Hopheeeaaaad. It is Marty, what is left of Marty, a face and open mouth and she's just able to get her partner's attention and pull her own finger across her throat and then point at the men at her bar.

Hophead glurts an affirmative sound and reaches for Fekete and vines slither around the man's drinking arm and stabs into it slipping between forearm bones and curling around them and spreading them and Fekete howls as Hophead pulls the man's forearm bones wide, popping ends out of Fekete's wrist so his hand dangles and his beer glass falls to the floor, and he screeches no no no I just wanna drink your shit, man, come on! Bellinger and Ashton are gone by the time Hophead opens Fekete's gut to see foamy still-cold beer spill out of him and run to a drain in the old factory floor.

Hophead drops him, makes a triumphant noise and turns to the empty place and speaks.

"Hophead will meet this ... Mouthfeel. And we shall see."

Its sinister laugh echoes among the brewkettles.

GOT
STEAMPUNK
MAGIC?
WORLDOFTHEFEY.COM

STEVEN MOHAN, JR.

Long-time professional writer Steven Mohan, Jr. makes his first appearance in these pages with this really fun comic-book-focused story. I found it hard to imagine that Steven hasn't been in these pages before, so he and I are fixing that now and with a few more stories in near future issues.

As a former Naval officer, Steven has professionally published more a half million words of military science fiction, including the BattleTech *novel* A Bonfire Of Worlds.

He has sold original fiction to markets as diverse as Interzone, Polyphony, *and* Paradox, *as well as several DAW original anthologies. His short stories have won honorable mention in* The Year's Best Science Fiction *and* The Year's Best Fantasy And Horror *and he has been nominated for the Pushcart Prize.*

ORIGIN STORY

STEVEN MOHAN, JR.

Did you ever read comic books as a kid? I did. Hundreds of them. *Thousands* of them. Not graphic novels. Not beautiful books with lush color published in trade paper. Not Frank Miller's *The Dark Knight Returns* or any of that gorgeous volume's many descendants. No, I'm talking thirty-two pages of haphazardly inked newsprint held together with *staples*. Ads for X-ray specs and Sea-Monkeys in the back.

Comic books.

I used to read them at two o'clock in the morning, sitting cross-legged under the covers, my sheets a tent, the flashlight's glow a bubble of light in the darkness, summer cicadas buzzing outside my window, their strange alien hum the only soundtrack to the Flash and *Action Comics* and *Detective Comics*. The Silver Surfer and the Green Lantern. X-Men and Iron Man and Spiderman. I loved them all. Marvel *and* DC.

Mom never understood why I was always so tired the next day.

My favorites?

Well, there was Superman. The Man of Steel. Truth, Justice, and the American Way. When I was a kid I believed in all that. If we try hard enough good can triumph.

Maybe a part of me *still* believes that.

Then there was the Batman. The Dark Knight. The Detective. Somehow he descended into Gotham's filthy underbelly and emerged clean. I never understood how Bruce Wayne accomplished that trick. I must have read four hundred funny books trying to find out.

But my favorite was the Fantastic Four.

It wasn't their powers that won me over. It was their *family*. I didn't have much of a family growing up. No dad. Mom always working. Me and my sister and brother coming home to a small, silent apartment. I would have traded my left nut for Sue Storm and her brother Johnny, the Human Torch. The Thing, the tough older brother who would always stand up for you. And most of all the dad. Reed Richards.

I always wanted a dad.

Comic books were a poor substitute for a *real* dad.

But they were all I had.

Anyway, read enough superhero comics and you'll come across origin stories. The tales of how our heroes won their powers. Maybe they grew to manhood beneath a yellow sun. Or they witnessed the murder of their parents on a dark, dirty Gotham street. Or they were bit by a radioactive spider.

A lot of superpowers were conferred by gamma rays, that

exotic radiation beyond ready human understanding. Exposure to gamma made us into mutants. Made us into freaks.

Made us into *heroes*.

That's the comic book understanding of gamma-ray showers.

The truth is somewhat different.

———

I'm sitting on one of those folding lawn chairs. You know what I mean, one of those horrors made out of nylon strapping stretched over a frame of bent aluminum tubing and as comfortable as a middle seat on Frontier Airlines. Anyway, it beats sitting on the ground which here is square-cut bedrock. Not exactly good for the ol' back.

It's dark down here, as black as a...

Well.

A mineshaft.

We're deep enough underground that no photons can penetrate, which is kind of the point. Since the gamma-ray source in Sagittarius let go, photons are not humanity's friend.

Anyway, there's no light save for the soft radiance of my iPad.

What am I reading?

Comics, of course. What else?

I'm not reading comics on the internet. There is no more internet. Humanity's collective memory has been burned away by a high-energy flux of radiation that makes an EMP look like a playful prank. Perhaps if we'd had more warning we could have saved that vast data storehouse. Even a tiny fraction of it. But, no. It's all gone. All I have to read is what I happened to have downloaded when the disaster hit.

It's the middle of the night—though when you live in a mineshaft concepts of day and night are mostly academic distinctions—and most of the refugees are sleeping.

Not me.

I like to read in the middle of the night. It's a habit I picked up when I was a kid. Though there are no cicadas outside my window. There *is* no window. And all the cicadas are dead. As dead as the internet.

My bladder's full, so I get up to piss. You probably think we've set up latrines, and we have, but I don't see the point of using them. There are miles and *miles* of mineshafts down here. There's the soft, trickling *hiss* that is the sound of relief, I put Little Roy away, and I zip back up. Then I move my wretchedly uncomfortable lawn chair down the mineshaft until I can no longer smell urine and go back to reading.

Easy.

"Mr. Hunter?"

A woman's voice swims out of the mineshaft darkness. There's a tired sort of panic threaded through that high-pitched voice, a jagged fear.

I look up from my dwindling supply of comic books and see Amber Holland. Mrs. Holland is pretty now. Before the Sagittarius gamma-ray burstar put a severe crimp in human civilization she must have been *beautiful*. Lovely hair the color of dark gold, cornflower eyes, the faintest spray of freckles across a pert nose, breasts high and firm.

You know, if you like that kind of thing.

Anyway, now the gold hair is greasy and lank, her skin sallow, those pretty eyes sitting in cups of bruised flesh, her white cotton blouse pitted out. The end of the world is tough on personal grooming standards.

"Yes?" I say.

"Mr. Hunter, I need your help."

I glance at the white-gold wedding band on her left ring finger. The man who had gone with that ring had been a pilot for United flying the DIA-LAX route when the burstar had showered the solar system with hard gamma.

I wonder what it had been like in the cockpit of his 757 when the first flash of gamma hit. All the computers suddenly going down, radios dead, navigation screens flickering to black, ventilation fans coasting down. Had they panicked as they had lost their fly-by-wire controls? Had they tried to reestablish hydraulic control of their flaps as their ship nosed down, heading for the ground like a thrown lance caught in gravity's parabolic embrace?

Probably not.

Probably everyone aboard the aircraft was dead when it began its final descent. The air is thin at thirty thousand feet. It doesn't offer a lot of shielding from horrific extra-solar extinction-level events.

Probably everyone was dead before they hit the ground.

Dead or dying.

I try to swallow in a mouth that tastes metallic and foul. This is why I don't talk to the other refugees. Who wants to think about this?

Not me.

I'm reading *The Flash* #175 in which Superman and the Flash are forced to race to the end of the Milky Way and back. It's not the best issue ever published by DC, but it is all I have and once I've read it, I'll be one comic book closer to the end. I don't want to stop in the middle. I sigh and look up. "I'm not sure how I—"

"Benny's missing."

Benny's her son. Fourteen. And just as dumb as any teenager.

Look, I'm not *totally* heartless. The kid has lost his dad. And he's living in the deep underground like a Morlock in the classic comic book version of H.G. Wells' *The Time Machine.* Sure, it sucks.

But I don't see what *I* can do about it.

"Why don't you wake some of the others. Organize a search party. I'm sure you'll find—"

She holds her right arm out toward me, the pale, delicate skin of her inner arm caught in my iPad's soft glow. She runs her perfectly manicured nails down her forearm. The skin, delicate as tissue paper, comes loose and sloughs off.

Bad.

That is bad.

Man, why do I *talk* to people?

"I've been throwing up blood," she whispers.

Even in the soft glow of my tablet, her eyes are diamond-bright.

She is dying. *Of course,* she is dying. Amanda Holland and her boy had been cleaning out the basement when the burstar erupted. That's the only reason she's even lasted *this* long. But she had caught enough gamma to give her radiation sickness. And even if she somehow rides *that* out, new and exotic cancers would be breeding in her cells like mosquito larvae in a pool of warm, stagnant water.

Cancer will probably get us all in the end, energetic photons ripping apart our genes and causing DNA transcription errors.

Maybe we could self-administer chemo. Maybe some of us will survive.

Maybe there will be enough survivors to reproduce.

Maybe.

But even if there are survivors, Amanda Holland won't be one of them. Not if she is at the throwing-up-blood stage of things.

No wonder Benny had taken a powder. He'd lost his dad.

And now his mom.

I *still* don't see what I could do about it.

But whatever Amber Holland wants from me I will try to give her. I guess I will see who won the race between Superman and the Flash later.

Except...

She looks like your standard Republican hausfrau to me. Probably is. Husband was a pilot, probably ex-Air Force. Or ex-Navy. And Colorado Springs is chock-full of Republicans. Why would a conservative housewife come to *me* for help?

"Why me, Mrs. Holland? Why would you want me to help with your son?"

She glances into the darkness as if the answer to my question is hidden in the lightless depths of the Earth.

"We used to live in a world where the winners were the people who locked in their mortgages when the prime was low," she tells the darkness. "The people who bought index funds and understood dollar-cost averaging."

She shakes her head, still talking into the black. "Not anymore. *Now* we live in the midst of apocalypse. We live in a world where fire rains from the sky."

Finally, she turns to look at me.

"Now we live in a comic-book world. And I think you might just have the best chance of making it through that world alive."

I haul myself up out of the lawn chair. I'm a big man, five-ten and two-fifty. I know, I know. Too much BK. Too much Pizza Hut. Too much Mickey D's. Of course, now that's it the end of the world I have a lot of reserve fat. While everyone else is starving to death, I'll merely be slimming down.

"What do you want from me?" I ask, trying to be kind.

"You showed up late." Her eyes are intent on my face.

I shrug. "Twenty-five was jammed."

And it had been. Everyone had been trying to get out of Denver, to get to the mountains, to shelter in one of the abandoned mines near Leadville. Most people hadn't made it. They had died in their Hondas and Teslas and Ford F150s, throwing their guts up in bumper-to-bumper traffic. Their panic had turned I-25 South into a frozen river of steel and glass.

"But you made it," she whispers. "You still made it. You were the last one to make it."

I say nothing.

I don't want to say anything. I don't even want to think about it. I just want to sit on my uncomfortable chair and read my comic books. Is that really too much to ask?

"You're a mutant," she says.

I shake my head. "You've read too many comic books."

Which, let me tell you, is a sentence I *never* expected to ever cross my lips.

"You're lying."

"I know you're upset, Mrs. Holland." I try to be as nice as possible. I know she is heartbroken over her dead husband. I know she is worried about her missing son. I know she is worried about leaving him alone in this terrible new world.

"But let me explain how mutation works. Random forces —radiation, chemicals, something else—scrambles the nuclear DNA in one of our cells. Usually, the change isn't viable and the cell can't reproduce. Or it *does* reproduce, but it's inferior to the original design and the body destroys it."

"But the mutation might be favorable," she insists. Her face looks very pale in the soft wash of light, her eyes sunken.

I shrug. "It *might* be. Probably not, though. If you take a cup of paint and throw it on the *Mona Lisa*, you *might* improve the painting—but you'll *probably* make it worse. Mostly mutations won't do anything. If they occur in our junk DNA, they won't affect the organism, at all, because the organism doesn't use those sections of DNA to express proteins. Those mutations will be irrelevant. And what few changes that *are* relevant will be harmful."

"But *some* mutations will be favorable."

"Okay, maybe. Maybe my children would have lower bad cholesterol." Not that *I* would ever have children. "But I'm not going to get superpowers. Gamma radiation isn't going to turn me into the Incredible Hulk. It's not going to turn me into Mr. Fantastic."

"You're wrong," she says.

"I'm not."

"You *are*."

"How can you even say that?" I ask exasperated.

She looks at me with those wounded eyes. "Because I can read your mind."

———

I stare at her. After a moment I realize my jaw is hanging open and I close it with an audible *clack.*

I shake my head. "You can't really—"

"You're gay," she says. "You keep that fact to yourself, but I can see it in your mind. You're gay."

Okay so she is good at reading people and maybe I haven't been quite as careful as I thought. Maybe I hadn't stared at her breasts enough or something. The eyes of straight men seem to be inevitably drawn to a woman's rack. It's a fact of nature, like a compass finding magnetic north. I guess I just can't fake it. I just don't *care.*

"You *did* look at my breasts," she says. "And you thought something like, They're nice—if you like that sort of thing."

Oh, *shit!*

That *had* been what I had thought.

"The odds against such a radical mutation taking hold—"

"Are what?" She cuts me off. "A thousand to one? A *million* to one?"

"More."

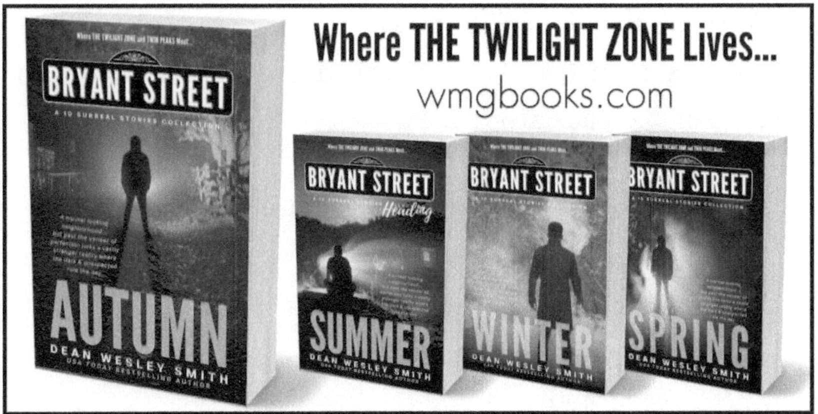

"Before the burstar exploded there were eight *billion* humans living on planet Earth. If the odds are a thousand to one, that means eight *million* mutants. At a million to one, we'd still have eight *thousand* mutants. I'm just a housewife, Mr. Hunter, but I can do math."

I turn that over in my mind. How many cans of paint would you have to throw on the *Mona Lisa* before you made an improvement?

Would eight billion be enough?

Her eyes brim with tears. "I can read my son, Mr. Hunter." Her voice is choked. Just the sound of it squeezes my heart. "He's desperate. Desperate to save *me*." She clenches her right hand into a fist and pounds it against the darkness. "I can *feel* it."

I say nothing.

What can I possibly say?

A tear spills out of her right eye and draws a crystalline track down her cheek. "I'm worried that he might try to make a run to a hospital to find medicine. To help *me*."

There's a chance—a *small* chance—that might actually work. If you timed it right. If you left when Sagittarius was on the other side of the planet. If you timed it right, before the Archer rotated back around.

If you were lucky.

How many of us had been lucky lately?

Dumb teenager.

I almost ask her what she wants *me* to do about it.

But I know what she wants. I *know.*

I can't read minds.

But still.

I know.

"Can't promise anything." Now *I* am all choked up. "But I will try."

She is crying harder now, tears streaming down her cheeks, her left nostril bubbling with snot, that pretty face made ugly by her grief, but she gives me a small nod. Mrs. Amber Holland—widow and mother—says two words so quiet that I can't hear them even in the stillness of that dark and still place.

But I read the words on her lips.

"Thank you," she says. "Thank you, Mr. Hunter."

———

Here's how human civilization ends. Not as a result of nuclear war. Not climate change. Not COVID. Not even an asteroid strike. Our doom lay thousands of light-years away. There was nothing we could do about it. *Nothing*.

Not very satisfying, right?

It takes away all our agency.

We've been hurtling towards our doom for hundreds of years. Thousands of years.

Millions of years.

When our ancestors were hunting mammoths across the North American tundra it was already too late. Our fate was *already* sealed.

That's not how *I* would write the comic book.

The villain of the piece is GRB 310629D, the fourth gamma-ray burst observed on June 29th, 2031.

Before GRB 310629D erupted it was a Wolf-Rayet star in

Sagittarius. The exemplar of WR stars is the blue supergiant Eta Carinae, a binary system that lies, thankfully, some 7,500 light-years from Earth.

The WR in Sagittarius was a little closer.

It just happened to be collinear with the Sun and Pi Sagittarii, which is just a fancy way of saying that all three stars were in a line. Pi Sagittarii—known as Albaldah by all the cool kids—lies 520 light-years from us. We don't *know* how far away the GRB origin point is. Farther than 520 light-years, certainly. But how much farther? A thousand light-years? Two thousand? *Five thousand?* No one knows for sure. No one really *can* know.

Even if any astronomers *had* survived.

The bottom line is that we don't know anything about the nameless star that destroyed our world. Albaldah shielded the WR in Sagittarius from view, like a fat man blocking out someone behind him.

We don't understand *that* part of the origin story.

It might not seem like it, but we were actually lucky in several ways. The fact that Albaldah was between us and the GRB may have blocked out a part of the gamma blast. And there was a precursor event before the main gamma burst, which gave some people a chance to get under cover.

But there were ways in which we were unlucky, too. The D eruption is classified by astronomers as an ultra-long gamma-ray burst—an eruption lasting longer than 10,000 seconds. GRB 310629D lasted for longer than *four* hours.

You think climate change is bad for the ecosystem!

Probably the gamma has passed, but there's an afterglow— no kidding, that's what they call it—that follows the original eruption. Phase one of the afterglow is energetic X-rays that can kill you just as dead as hard gamma. So, yeah. Still a bad idea to go topside.

And that's most of what needs to be said about current events.

Well, except for one postscript.

The actual *name* of humanity's executioner.

Every supervillain needs a cool moniker, right?

We don't have a formal name for the WR star in Sagittarius because astronomers never knew it was there until it erupted.

Most people—meaning the handful of survivors living like moles down in the darkness—have invented names for the nameless star in Sagittarius. *Death Star* is popular. So is *Doom Star. Armageddon Star. Apocalypse Star.* I suppose *Wormwood* was inevitable. A handful of people in love with irony like *Star of Bethlehem.* Then there are all the names that invoke the deity. *God's Wrath. God's Fury. God's Love.*

God's Judgement.

I find that last one the most chilling. Wolf-Rayets are young creatures as stars go, only a few million years old. But a few million years is elderly by the standards of human evolutionary history. It's a good order of magnitude older than *Homo sapiens sapiens*. Had God really judged the human race and found us wanting before we'd even climbed down out of the trees and taken our first faltering steps across the African savannah?

That's cold, man.

Fucking cold.

But then I suppose we live in a chilly universe.

———

I find the boy at the mine's east-face entrance. He's sitting twenty feet back from the square cut into the mountain's flank, far enough back that he's safe from the gamma or X-ray or whatever God's Judgement is showering down upon the Earth, but close enough that he is illuminated by the scatter of the dawn's light.

Benny Holland's not a terrible-looking kid, a little heavy-set, his round face framed by curly dark blond hair. He looks like his mom, his nose small, his eyes blue. His face is turned away from me.

He's looking out at the morning.

It's a cool day for early summer, maybe fifty, but then it's always cooler in the mountains. The entrance looks like a rectangle cut out of the darkness. That little piece of geometry is framed right and left by Ponderosa pines and Douglas firs, the trees' needles already starting to brown. Scragly scrub oak crowd the bottom of the picture giving way to bare earth near the center. And above the dying trees and the barren world?

The sky.

The beautiful, deadly sky as blue as a robin's egg.

I stand there for a minute, hot and tired and frustrated, smelling the stink of my own sweat. Then I go over and sit down beside the boy. For a long time, the two of us sit there together staring out at the world in silence.

Finally, I say, "You can't go out there, Benny."

"I know," he says, grievously offended. "I'm not *stupid*."

Ah, to be a teenager.

"Even if the gamma wavefront has passed, there's going to be X-ray. It'll fry you down to your bones."

I think about all the people I'd seen who had died in their cars on Twenty-Five.

He rolls his eyes. It's an impressive eye-roll. If the Olympics had an event for adolescent contempt he would have at least won the bronze.

Maybe even the *silver*.

"The terrible thing about radiation is that it's invisible."

He gives a derisive little snort.

"You can't smell it. Or *taste* it. You sure as hell can't *see* it. Doesn't matter how long you sit here looking, you can never be sure it's safe."

He drags a forearm across his face, hiding his eyes.

"It's my mom," he sobs.

It's like a punch to the gut.

I'd never had a dad.

But I *did* have a mom.

What kid wouldn't risk everything to save his mom?

"Okay," I say, my voice rough with emotion. "Maybe I can help."

With a grunt, I haul myself to my feet. I walk towards that rectangle of light, that doorway into a dead world.

The boy ignores me at first, but when I draw to within five or six feet of the entrance he looks up. "What are you doing?"

I ignore him. I keep walking.

"Hey, Mr. Hunter. Mr. Hunter, *stop!*"

But I don't stop.

I walk right up to the edge.

My heart hammers in my chest, blood throbbing in my temples and my wrists. The air tastes coppery and foul.

I'm not afraid of the energetic photons God's Judgement is showering down on the world. As Benny's mom had guessed, I have a way to protect myself against that deadly downpour. My journey along I-25 had taught me I could survive *that*.

What terrifies me is having to face a dead world.

Earth is a graveyard in winter, the trees' limbs bare, the ground cold and hard. I'm not sure I could endure all we have lost.

It would break me.

I have the sudden urge to find my lawn chair and dive back into my comic books. The compulsion is almost over-powering.

Instead, I toss my iPad down on the mine's dirt floor.

I *will* face up to the dead world.

For the boy.

Maybe that's what fathers do. Maybe that's what fathers *are*.

They do the hard thing.

For their children.

I close my eyes.

And call water to me.

I can *feel* it, molecules of water vapor suspended in the air, the water in clouds high above, a fountain of water gushing out of a fountain sheared from the ground by a car collision, water in pipes and culverts and swimming pools and ditches and retaining pools and ponds and reservoirs and brown tannin-filled mountain creeks, even the faint mist in the boy's exhalations. I feel it. *All* of it.

Like Benny's mother, I have been touched by gamma, only I hadn't gotten the ability to read minds.

I had gotten *this*.

I call water to me.

And it comes, drop by drop, molecule by molecule, until the mine's entrance is capped by a hemisphere of shimmering, crystalline water twenty or thirty feet thick.

Benny is on his feet, just staring, his mouth a round, shocked O.

His easy, teenaged derision has been replaced by total astonishment.

By *wonder*.

"It's safe," I say. "Water is a good shielding material against certain kinds of radiation."

"Are you *sure?*"

Now Benny isn't a world-weary adolescent. Now he is a scared kid.

"Sure thing, champ."

He just stares at me, his mouth still open.

"Look, I can't promise we can save your mom. But we can find meds for the pain and the nausea. As for the rest of it... Well, we can try."

I hold my hand out to him.

He swallows, his Adam's apple bobbing. Then his face hardens and he gives a determined nod.

He takes my hand.

And we step outside, beneath our half-dome of water.

It is like being inside a tear.

It is like being inside sorrow.

———

Amber Holland had thought we were living in a comic-book world.

I'm not so sure.

If this *were* a comic-book world Benny and I would have found the meds we needed to save his mom's life. After a decent interval of mourning for her late husband, she would have fallen in love with me and we would have formed a new family that would have strode into a new world.

If this were a comic-book world.

The truth is somewhat different.

I don't think Amber Holland ever expected to survive her gamma exposure. What I realize now is that she wasn't asking me to use my power to retrieve the meds that would save her life. No, she was asking me to look after her son after she was gone.

That's what I agreed to whether I really understood it or not.

That's what she thanked me for.

I never had a father growing up. No one to teach me how to be a *man*. No one to teach me how to be a dad. Maybe you think a lost, heartbroken boy deserves someone better than a fat, gay comic-book aficionado. But this is the world the gamma-ray shower has left us. *This* is what we have.

My father gave up on my family.

But good fathers don't give up. They do the hard thing for their children.

So *I* won't give up on the boy.

The water thing is just a parlor trick.

My real superpower is not giving up on the boy.

TODD MCCAFFREY

New York Times bestselling writer, Todd McCaffrey, makes his first appearance in these pages with this really twisted short story that answers the question in the title.

Todd has written over forty books. He writes both science fiction and fantasy, including eight in the Dragonriders of Pern® universe. the six-book Canaris Rift Series, the on-going Steamworld series (The Steam Walker, The Steam Spy), the new LA Witch series, and the Twin Soul Series in collaboration with the Winner Twins.

Check out all of Todd's new work at toddmccaffrey,com.

WHY I SHOT MY CAR

TODD MCCAFFREY

"Lieutenant," a uniformed cop interrupted Harris' meditation over a computer display.

"Unh?"

"Got another one for you," the cop said, dropping a vid-disk on the officer's desk. Beside it, with a louder thunk he dropped a pistol wrapped in a plastic bag. "The guy's confessed, it's on the disk."

Harris picked up the gun. "And this?"

"That's the weapon," the cop replied. "Ballistics got a positive match." With a snort, he added, "Five bullets."

"Five bullets?"

"Yeah, a real amateur."

"Where is he?" Harris asked, fingering the vid-disk.

"He's in Holding."

"Okay, I'll get on it." He lifted the vid-disk. "This a tape or an image?"

"Image," the cop said. "The guy insisted on it."

"Oh, great!"

A vid-disk image was a mental copy of the thoughts and actions of a suspect—a mental duplicate of a slice of the suspect's life.

A mental image was more than admissible evidence—it was sufficient grounds to release a suspect if the reviewing officer so decided.

However, reviewing a mental image invariably caused disorientation and pain. Harris' hands went to his head in anticipation.

The cop grunted sympathetically and turned to leave, "I gotta get back on the beat, lieutenant."

"Hey, wait!" Harris called when he took as closer look at the disk. "There's no index on this!"

"Yeah," the officer said with a frown, "the computer didn't assign any Emotional Index to this tape."

Harris groaned. It was normal for the analyzing computers to assign an Emotional Index on any confession using mental images. There had been that case of the poor cop who had reviewed a serial killer's confession...

When the computer did not assign an EI it either meant that the material had no significant impact on a viewer or the system was incapable of assigning a value.

Harris pocketed the disk and headed to the Viewing Rooms—a special set of rooms for officers to review vid-disk images under supervision.

The duty sergeant assigned him Room Three and Officer Mendez. Harris had worked with Mendez before—they had no need to exchange words.

There were several chairs in the room and a table. On the table was a computer display, keyboard and vid-disk drive. One chair was different from the rest—plush, upholstered and fitted with a Viewing Helmet. Harris took that chair and pulled the helmet down over his head. Mendez lounged in another chair.

"Ready?" Mendez said, inserting the vid-disk.

"Shoot." Harris replied.

The darkness of helmet blurred and was replaced with the light of early morning. Harris felt the usual disorientation as his 'eyes' adjusted to the visual perception of another person and he *became* the suspect.

———

Monday. And I was late for work. Bad enough that the kids were causing trouble but Molly and I had had another fight. It was sort of a relief to get out of the house and hop in my car. I should have known better.

"'Morning, Jenny."

"Good morning, Mark." Jenny replied quickly enough.

I put the key in the ignition and turned it. Nothing. I tried again. Then I realized—silly me! I hadn't stuck in the clutch. Still nothing. "Jenny, what's up?"

"I'm not starting."

"I noticed—why?" I looked at the gauges—nothing seemed wrong.

"I'm five hundred and two-tenth miles overdue for a service."

I blew out my breath. We'd had this argument for the past week. "I know that, Jenny, and I promise I'll get you in as soon as I can."

"You could have done it Saturday," Jenny said. "Or Sunday."

"I was busy Saturday," I said. "*You* know."

"Yes, you and the family went to the Mall," Jenny said. "And little Jeremy dropped his ice cream cone in the back seat—"

"We cleaned it up!"

"You *tried*. There's still dried ice cream on the carpet! And I haven't been washed in *ages*!"

"We'll get to it, I promise. Besides, what's a little dirt?" The words slipped out before I could catch myself.

"A little dirt? A *little* dirt?" My car responded indignantly. "It's been a whole month since I was last washed. Do you know what that dust does to my aerodynamics? I'm losing over half a mile an hour in top speed and burning a tenth of a gallon extra every thousand miles and *you* say—'a little dirt'! Don't you care about the environment, about your children?"

"Of course I do," I said. "But you can't seriously expect me to believe that not being washed for a month is going to make a big impact on anything. After all, it rained last week."

"And did you notice that my right windshield wiper is frayed?"

"No." I glanced at the right side of the windshield for signs of wiper tracks. "In fact, I don't see anything wrong."

"No, of course not," Jenny said primly. "That's because I compensated. But how long do you think I can go on like this?"

"Don't worry, old gal, we won't let you break down or anything."

"Won't you?" she demanded sarcastically. "Have *you* seen the color of my oil?"

"Well no, but the oil light's not on," I said. "And didn't we get you that special long-life oil anyway?"

"That's not the point." Jenny snapped. "My oil's dirty and you just *know* what that could mean—poorer lubrication, worse heat dissipation and—" Jenny sniffed "—early breakdowns!"

"Okay, okay," I said soothingly. "Don't get upset. We'll get you serviced, I already promised. But Jenny, I'm going to be late for work."

"I'll book an appointment. We can go in today at ten."

"No good. I'm going to be in meetings all day."

"How about tomorrow?"

"Same."

"Are you sure?" Jenny asked with suspicion. "Wait a minute! *Wait* a minute! I just checked with your appointments computer - you're going to be free tomorrow from twelve until one."

"That's *lunchtime*, Jenny!"

"So? What's more important, your stomach or my safety?"

Jenny demanded. "Do you realize that my right front tire pressure is half a pound too low? I've compensated with the left rear pressure, of course, but it's just too much, I tell you, too much!"

"I really have to eat, Jenny," I told her. "Anyway, tomorrow's a meeting with some of the boys at work, it wouldn't be on my appointments computer because it's a private deal."

"Oh, is it?" Jenny said. "With the boys? Or maybe it's not. You aren't fooling around, are you Mark?" There was a pause. "What about that trip we took three weeks ago Wednesday after work?"

"Huh?"

"Yes. Didn't we go to your secretary's apartment?"

I could feel heat rising in my cheeks. "That was to drop off her briefcase!"

"Oh, was it?" Again Jenny paused. "The house computer tells me that you and Molly were fighting again. It had to turn the de-ionizer up all the way just to reduce the tension."

"That was the kids!"

"Oh, certainly," Jenny agreed dubiously. "And what did the kids do?"

"They were fighting, okay? And I don't see where you, a common appliance—"

"Common! Common? I assure you that I am one of the finest automobiles that money can buy today—"

"Sure!" I snorted. Another mistake.

Jenny's tone was pouting—"Well, I would be if you would take care of me! My differential's a hundredth of an inch low on oil! A whole hundredth! And my right rear wheel bearing needs greasing!"

She sobbed, "You just don't care!"

"Of course I care. If I didn't I wouldn't have bought you."

"You're just going to use me and throw me away!" Jenny protested. "And you won't even get me proper servicing! Well, I won't start, do you hear me! I won't start. You're going nowhere!"

I groaned. "C'mon Jenny! We had this argument yesterday!"

"And I didn't start then, did I?"

"That's right," I said, "we decided we could do without the extra loaf of bread. But today I have to get to work."

"You should have thought of that before you went to the Mall."

"Huh?"

"I warned you then. I told you that you were driving me beyond my limitations—"

"Sure, but—"

"—and now you've done it! I'm not going anywhere unless it's a service station!"

"Listen, you pompous collection of chips and metal—I've got to get to work because if I don't I can't *pay* for your service so you'd just better start up right now before my boss docks my pay!"

"Can't pay? Can't pay?" Jenny's tone switched from sarcastic to horrified between the first and the second question.

"That's right. Remember when we took Jeremy to the hospital?"

"Yes-s," Jenny said.

"Well, we hadn't counted on it and it's ruined our monthly budget."

"How can I know you're telling the truth?"

"Why the hell do I have to justify myself to you?" I roared back, turning the key viciously in the ignition. "Start, dammit! Start right now or I'll—"

"What? What more could you do to me?" She wailed with all the tone of a wronged appliance.

"I'll take you apart!" I shouted, hoping to shock her, twisting the key in the ignition provocatively.

"Hah! You can barely change a flat! I remember the day when you drove me over all that glass and I had to talk you through, step by step—"

"No you didn't! I could have read the manual but you refused to let me!" I banged the glove compartment open, pulled out the manual and waved it at the dash.

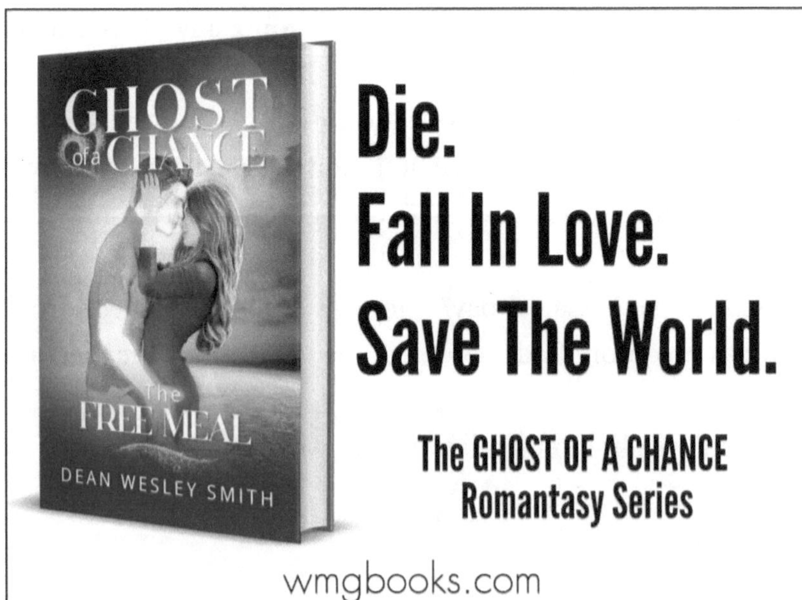

"What's up? Robbers? Do you need some protection? Are we going *shooting*?" The voice was a husky alto and belonged to the pistol I'd bought several years back when I'd spent a very uncomfortable time in one of the more troubled neighborhoods. I'd uncovered it when I pulled the manual out of the glove compartment.

"No, nah! I just wanted to show Jenny here the damned manual."

"So you've got the manual, so what?" Jenny snapped.

I started rifling it, found the table of contents. "There's an override code here somewhere."

"You wouldn't dare!" Jenny declared. "You'd endanger your family and yourself."

"Just watch me."

"I can't let you!"

"Here it is—page ten." I flicked over to page ten and read: "'In case of emergencies, the artificial intelligence of your machine may be disabled with the phrase— *<Use machine's name>*, I don't feel well.'"

I shot a grin at the car's dash. "Jenny, I don't feel well!" And turned the key.

Nothing. I tried again. "Jenny, I don't feel well!"

"This is not an emergency!" Jenny said with a huff. "I won't let you disable me!"

"You won't! What do you mean you won't? Who puts gas in you? Who pays for your repairs? Who's *still* paying you off?"

"In situations like this, it never hurts to have a handy persuader." The gun in the glove compartment pointed out.

"You butt out!" Jenny and I shouted back simultaneously.

I continued, "Now look, Jenny, I've got to get to work. I've told you why. We'll get your service scheduled as soon as possible—"

"As soon as you can afford, you mean."

"That's what I meant!"

"And when will that be?" Jenny said. "Jeremy's trip to the hospital cost an awful lot, it'll be three point four-five months before you've paid off the bills for that visit—"

"How'd you know?" I demanded, horrified.

"I accessed your home computer records. It says that you've promised to have the plumbing fixed as well. And Jeremy's current health record indicates that—"

"He broke a leg, fer crying out loud!"

"He'll break something else within the next six months," Jenny stated. "I'm not programmed to tell you how to raise your kids but I think that you and your wife would be capable of ensuring a lower accident rate among them—or maybe you don't get them serviced regularly, either!"

"You don't service humans!"

"Maybe somebody should!"

"Maybe somebody should *sell* you!"

Jenny was shocked to silence. Finally she said to me, "You can't, you still owe the bank."

"Well, you're no good to me if you won't start!"

"Have you considered a little 'friendly' persuasion?" the gun suggested in sultry tones.

"What the hell." I grabbed the gun. "Okay, start!"

"You don't scare me!" Jenny said. "You probably don't even know how to use that thing, anyway!"

That was it—I pulled the trigger. The *boom* reverberated throughout the car and left me deaf.

"Hah, you missed!" Jenny shouted. "I'm calling the police!"

"No, you're not!" I shouted, firing again—*blam-blam!*

"No! No, you're ruining my circuits!"

"Start!"

"I can't!"

"You mean you won't!" And I let her have it again and again. The last time I shattered the windshield and it caved in on top of me, cut my face.

"Now start!"

"Your target is destroyed." the gun said. "You destroyed it with the fourth shot. You also punctured the radiator, the battery, the right front tire, and the oil pump. I don't recommend firing again or starting the car."

She paused, adding breathlessly—"Will you clean me now, you big brute of a man?"

———

The image faded and blackness returned. Harris lifted the helmet.

"You okay?" Mendez asked.

"Sure."

"So what do you think?"

"Five shots. He didn't fire all six." Harris picked up the gun still secure in the baggy.

Dropping it back on the table, he said, "There's not a jury in the world that would convict him. Let him go."

————

Muffled by the bag, the gun's sultry voice could just barely be heard, "*Oooh!* I feel *so* used! Who's going to clean me *now?*"

POKER BOY

Read all his adventures at

wmgbooks.com

DAVID H. HENDRICKSON

Full-time professional writer David H. Hendrickson has been a writer for many, many years, not only as a fiction writer, but writing thousands of sports articles. He knows writing. And he knows life.

With Dave, you never know what kind of story you will get, which as editor and fan of his work, I love. For example, this story I have no clue how to say anything about it. Dave can write twisted with the best of them.

Dave's short fiction has appeared in Best American Mystery Stories, Ellery Queen's Mystery Magazine, Heart's Kiss, *and numerous anthologies, including over a half dozen issues of* Fiction River *and just about every issue of this magazine so far. Check it all out at hendricksonwriter.com.*

MALE MONSOON

DAVID H. HENDRICKSON

It was raining men. Literally. Not metaphorically. Literally. Hundreds of them.

Men of all races, sizes, shapes, and ages. Black men, white men, Latin, Native American, and Asian. Tall, short, and in between. Gym rats with chiseled physiques, bodybuilders, and elite marathoners without an ounce of fat. Weekend athletes fighting the battle of the bulge and losing. Dad bods. Rotund couch potatoes. The morbidly obese. College boys, thirty-somethings, middle-aged men, and beyond. All the way to frail, white-haired senior citizens.

They came floating down from the sky. None of them crashlanding, which would have been ghastly. Instead they touched down softly. Stood there looking puzzled, empty-headed and befuddled, blinking their eyes of blue, brown, and green. Specific eye colors straight from romance novels: baby blue, electric blue, piercing blue, ice blue, amber, hazel, and chestnut brown. Chocolate, mud brown, charcoal gray, gun metal gray, slate gray, emerald green, forest green, jade green, and of course, black as coal.

For the majority of unattached women and gay men, the deluge would have been a bonanza. A cornucopia of opportunity. An embarrassment of riches.

Sophie McLanahan was a lesbian.

Not since the Biblical plague of locusts had the heavens rained down such an onslaught of unwanted pests.

They wore everything from expensively tailored dark suits and power ties to business casual to T-shirts and jeans to flannel pajamas to nothing but neon-colored gym shorts to… well… nothing at all, their you-know-what's flopping in the breeze.

Sophie, twenty-nine years old with short, auburn brown hair and an athletic build befitting her regular trips to the gym, stood transfixed, looking out the picture window of her modest suburban house on a quiet side street an hour north of Boston. She watched it all unfold with wide-eyed shock, followed by disgust, and then finally, horror.

At first, the precipitation amounted to little more than a light drizzle. Noticeable, of course. Impossible to miss. It was, after all, a drizzle of *men*. Shocking. At no other point in history had it *literally* rained men. But it began as just a sprinkling of them, most of them initially movie-star good-looking, floating slowly down from the clouds, drifting in the slight breeze, arms outstretched beatifically, coming to rest softly on the ground.

After a short time, though, the light drizzle became a steady drip, drip, drip. Men leaking out of the sky onto Sophie's lawn, driveway, and porch. One blond-haired, blue-eyed, bare-chested pretty boy landed and lay seductively sprawled on the hood of Sophie's year-old black Camry, parked nose-in in the driveway. Over and over, he combed his thick, luxurious hair with a glittering, bejeweled brush as if preparing for a photo shoot. A beaming smile and come-hither look came over his face.

Sophie wasn't coming hither.

A light thump sounded on the roof directly above her.

Sophie yelped. Spun around. Saw she was alone. At least for now.

She checked the front door to see that it was locked, then raced past the blank large-screen TV to the kitchen for the longest, sharpest knife she could find. Raced back and stared again through the picture window at the disgusting sight. She could practically smell a cloud of noxious cologne and after-shave leaking into the house.

The steady drip, drip, drip of men picked up its pace. And in sync, so too did the drumbeat on the roof above. Faster and faster. One repulsive sack of testosterone after another. Landing outside and echoing on the roof above.

Faster and faster until the pestilential precipitation became a torrential downpour, most of them now—not that it mattered to Sophie—at the opposite end of the aesthetic spectrum from the hunk with the hairbrush on the Camry's hood. One Dad bod after another. Not that it mattered, but the plague's Quality Assurance department had apparently sprung a leak.

They all just stood there, whether flabby or chiseled. All of them befuddled and useless. Typical men.

If only they would fall over, Sophie thought bizarrely.

Then she could stack them up neatly like cords of firewood. She couldn't burn them in the fireplace, of course. There was the obvious matter of ethics since these facsimiles of men might actually be human. She was no monster. But there was also the practical concern that even as mere facsimiles of men, these canisters of bottled up testosterone could easily explode. Who could she ever hire to clean up that mess?

As that ugly thought polluted her mind, the torrential downpour became a monsoon of men, pouring out of the sky in sheets so thick Sophie could barely make out the hunk still posing on the Camry's hood, combing his hair. Soon, every square inch of her lawn, porch, and driveway was covered with the vermin. There wasn't enough space for all of them, so they began landing one atop each other.

They all just stood there staring, even as more of their kind landed on top of them, draping themselves across their hosts' shoulders at all angles, eyes vacant, blinking mindlessly. Piling up haphazardly into mounds of flesh. Like trash at the town dump.

At the top of the picture window, a head suddenly appeared, upside down, its eyes wide and a frozen, upside-down grin on its lips.

Sophie yelped.

Slowly, the rest of its body slipped off the roof, first the shoulders, then the chest and torso, appearing impossibly close to her. As if in slow motion, the body dropped to the ground and landed with a hollow thud.

And then another followed, sliding off the roof, smiling all the way down. As if grateful to be blessed with her as its audience.

Was there no more room up on the roof either? Could the ten-year-old roof support all that weight? And what if it couldn't? Would dozens of men crash through the ceiling on top of her?

Sophie's stomach lurched at the thought.

When a momentary pause occurred in the onslaught of men, Sophie could suddenly see beyond her own front yard. She realized to her astonishment that none of the men were landing in the road, a lightly traveled side street fifty feet from her front door, or for that matter, across the street on her neighbor's lawn or empty driveway. Sophie craned her neck to see the other neighbors' yards and driveways. They, too, were free of this… this deluge of the male subspecies. Or whatever facsimile they might be.

They littered only Sophie's property. The toxic waste site was hers and hers alone.

Well, hers and her wife, Katie's. They owned this property. The two of them were stuck with this mess.

For better or for worse.

Sophie hadn't thought to call Katie because… well, mostly because Sophie had never been so shocked into paralysis in her entire life, but also because Katie was unreachable, on a flight halfway to Los Angeles on a business trip.

Sophie pulled her phone from her pocket and began to take rapid-fire photographs and videos of everything, proof of the impossible. The men piled up on the lawn, driveway, and porch. The ones hanging down from the roof. And her neighbors' perfectly clean yards.

All the while asking herself, *why is this only happening to me? To us?*

Why?

She stared across the street at the neighbors' clean lawns and driveways, then shrank in disgust at what stared back at her from her own front lawn, driveway, porch, and upside-down off the roof. But she kept clicking photographs. Checking every now and then to verify the smartphone's camera was seeing what she saw.

It was. Seeing the impossible.

From down the street to the left, a black SUV approached, then drove by but didn't stop or even slow down.

Sophie stared at tail lights disappearing in the distance. *How could that be? How could a driver fail to notice, neither slowing down at the stunning sight nor racing off in fear?*

Sophie grabbed the remote off the coffee table and turned on the TV. Or tried to.

The screen remained blank.

Sophie swallowed hard. Had the men outside disabled the connection? Perhaps accidentally by brute force of all that weight landing in the wrong spot. Or perhaps intentionally. Like in a horror movie come to life.

Sophie held back a scream. Her heart skipped a beat.

The TV came to life.

She stared at it wide-eyed, glanced back at the horror show out the picture window, then stared back at the TV. Had it only seemed slower than usual? Had she just been panicking? Sophie was pretty sure she knew the answer to those questions.

Forcing herself to breathe normally, or as normally as possible, she pressed the digits to pull up the twenty-four-hour news stations, one after another.

Nothing but the usual blather.

Then the local network affiliate. Surely, it would be interrupting the regularly scheduled programming with this breaking news.

Nothing.

Outside, lightning flashed, illuminating the darkened sky. Ear-splitting thunder crashed.

Wide-eyed, panicked faces of the men filled the lower half of the picture window. Then, hanging down from the roof above, others filled the upper portion of the window, too. As they slipped and fell off, they were replaced by others.

"Go away!" Sophie screamed, picking up the kitchen knife and waving it in warning even while recognizing its futility as a defense weapon should these hundreds of men somehow get inside. *"Go away!"*

Lightning brighter than Sophie had never seen flashed across the sky. Thunder boomed so loudly the house seemed to rock. Rain poured down from the heavens in sheets so thick Sophie could barely see outside the window.

Real rain. The old-fashioned kind. Water, sweet water, not male flesh.

The men began to melt. The rain drained first their features from their faces, then the faces themselves, and finally, all the rest of their bodies.

One after another, like a water coloring washed away by buckets of cleansing water, they faded and then disappeared.

Until finally, after a deluge of the most wonderful, old-fashioned, life-sustaining rain ever, the last of the men that had floated down from the clouds was gone.

Sophie waited for the longest time to be sure, then waited some more.

Outside, the thunder had fallen silent, the lightning flashed no more, and the skies were clear and suddenly cloudless. The rain was now mere puddles in the driveway and on the drenched lawn.

Gripping her kitchen knife and baring her teeth like a Rottweiler, Sophie poked her head out the front door.

The men were gone. All melted away. Off the porch, lawn, roof, and driveway. All of them, even the bare-chested pretty boy that had been laying on her Camry's hood, combing his pretty-boy blond hair.

All of them gone, leaving nothing behind but the cleansing flood of the water that had melted them away.

Wait until Katie sees this, Sophie thought as she pulled out her phone and pressed the flowery icon for Photos.

Sophie froze. She swiped at the photos and videos in disbelief.

They were gone.

Not the photos. The men that had rained down from the skies. She'd taken almost fifty photos and videos of them on the lawn, driveway, and hood of her car, checking to make sure she was getting the whole impossible picture, but now…

The photos showed nothing at all but the yard and driveway, barren of men, just as it had been yesterday and the day before that. And now, except for the drenching rain.

Sophie walked, as if in a dream, about the wet front lawn, sure she was smelling the cologne and aftershave left behind by the unwanted intruders, but seeing nothing to prove what she'd seen. Only proof that she was losing her mind.

There wasn't a single shred of evidence that for however many minutes this nightmare had lasted, the heavens had rained men. Onto her property—hers and Katie's—and theirs alone. Onto all of it. Hundreds of them.

Now she couldn't tell Katie. Didn't dare to. For better or for worse, sure. But saying anything about this would be a self-inflicted wound in their already imperfect relationship. A reason for Katie to give her a strange look and wonder.

No, Sophie knew there was no need to spill these particular beans. At least until a trip to her therapist made sense out of this… this… this, well, it had to be a hallucination, didn't it?

Sophie didn't believe in ghosts, werewolves, or vampires. She didn't believe in UFOs or any of the conspiracy theories. How could she ever believe in the heavens raining men?

Even if she'd seen it with her own eyes.

The memory suddenly came back to her of the black SUV driving by with all those men piled on her front lawn and in her driveway, but the SUV never slowed down. The people inside hadn't noticed a single thing.

Impossible.

If the men from the heavens had really been there. Which clearly, they hadn't.

Sophie had heard of LSD flashbacks for old-time hippies. She'd never taken LSD. But maybe this was an LSD flashback, hold the LSD. That was as good an explanation as any.

Sophie had to take this crazy, impossible afternoon with her to the grave. She really had no choice. Not even tell her therapist about it. For sure, not tell her therapist about it. Or Katie.

Sophie shook her head sadly, staring one last time at the useless photographs that she had been convinced showed the men who had rained down from the heavens.

She turned to head back inside. But stopped when out of the corner of her eye she saw something glitter.

Sophie turned back. Looked more closely.

At the hood of the Camry. Which appeared to have the slightest dent in the middle.

And the pretty boy's bejeweled hairbrush.

O'NEIL DE NOUX

O'Neil De Noux takes his amazing skills as one of the best writers of detective fiction working today and gives us another wonderful look at the realities of police work. Sometimes very harsh realities. The places and events and characters just come alive in O'Neil's powerful hands.

O'Neil has published about fifty novels with more coming regularly. His awards include The United Kingdom Short Story Prize, the Shamus Award (for best private eye fiction), the Derringer Award (for excellence in mystery short fiction) and Police Book of the Year.

Two of his stories have appeared in the prestigious Best American Mystery Stories *annual anthology and I noticed he had another in the recommended reading for this last year's volume. He won the Shamus for a story in 2020. You can find out a lot more about his work at his website oneildenoux.com.*

THE MAN WITH MOON HANDS

O'NEIL DE NOUX

Before the meat wagon arrived, LaStanza went to take a look at the body. He didn't need a flashlight. The bright moon shined directly into that dirty New Orleans alley. Just inside the alley, LaStanza passed a young patrolman with sandy hair explaining to the other policemen, "He had a gun."

The body was about half way down the dead end alley. LaStanza's partner, Paul Snowood, stood over it. Next to him, a crime lab technician was reloading his camera.

"Come see this," Snowood twanged. "Got him through the pump with one shot." In his cowboy hat, rope tie around the neck of his western shirt, brown jeans and snakeskin boots, Detective Snowood couldn't look more out of place if he tried.

"You sure you don't want me to take this?" LaStanza asked as he stepped up.

"You're up to your ass in murders already, boy, " Snowood

said. "This ain't nothin' but paperwork." Tilting his Stetson back, Snowood pointed to the body with his note pad and added, "Anyway, it looks like a good shootin'."

The body was on its side, legs straight out, arms contorted like soft pretzels. There were holes in the soles of both shoes and a worn spot on the man's jeans above the left knee. A stain of dark blood had gathered beneath the twisted torso. A small caliber, blue steel semi-automatic lay two feet from the man's head. It was a typical Saturday-night-special.

"You can handle the canvass for me, if you've a hankerin'."

"Sure," LaStanza said as he leaned over the body.

It was a white male, mid-twenties, about five feet - eight inches tall, one hundred and eighty pounds with frizzy brown hair and a large gunshot wound in the center of his chest. Stepping out of the way of the technician, LaStanza paused and looked back at the body. There was something familiar about it. That was when he saw the hands.

He found some empty soft drink cases a few feet away and sat on them as his partner and the technician began taking measurements. Tugging angrily on his moustache, LaStanza stared at the pallid hands, at the limp fingers that looked like white goldfish left out to rot, and remembered ...

———

Lastanza had been riding alone that night when the call came out.

"Headquarters—any Sixth District Unit. Signal 103M with a gun. 2300 block of Rousseau."

A disturbance on Rousseau Street involving a mental case

with a gun. There was only one appropriate thought: "Fuck Me!"

It was a typically busy night in the Bloody Sixth District. LaStanza was the only one available. He flipped on his blue lights, accelerated and made it to Rousseau in less than two minutes. He found a small gathering in the 2300 block, about a dozen people standing in the street in front of an alley between a large warehouse and a junk yard. He was surprised to see a white face in the crowd.

As he climbed out, the white face approached and pointed to the alley and said, "My son's in there with a twenty-five automatic. He's a mental patient." The man was tall and very thin and wore thick spectacles.

"What's his problem?" LaStanza asked the spectacles.

"He's crazy."

"Who gave him the gun?"

"I did. I mean it's mine."

Crazy? It ran in the family. Now it was LaStanza's problem. There was a loony-tune in an alley with a gun. LaStanza withdrew his stainless steel .357 Smith and Wesson and approached the alley. He could see the young man clearly, standing under a light near the side door of the warehouse.

The man paid no attention to LaStanza moving into the alley. Looking up at the sky, the loony-tune ran his left hand through his frizzy hair. In his right hand he held a small, blue steel automatic. He looked to be in his early twenties.

When he finally noticed LaStanza, he craned his neck forward and grinned. His large, bulbous eyes batted frantically at the approaching patrolman. He slowly raised the automatic, pointed it toward LaStanza, who ducked into the shadows.

The man went, "Zap. Zap." He followed this with a frightened laugh. His hand was shaking so hard, LaStanza thought the gun would fall.

The .357 magnum was cocked and pointed center on the man's chest.

"Put it down," LaStanza told the man as calmly as he could, "or I'll blow your brains out the back of your head." LaStanza's hands were steady, his voice flat and dry.

Then man laughed again as his gun slowly inched forward until he let it drop to the ground. Then he raised his hands and said, "You see these hands?" The man glared at the huge white digits at the end of his palms. "They're not my hands. They're moon hands!"

LaStanza moved forward, stepped on the automatic, holstered his magnum and slapped a handcuff across the loony's right wrist.

"These aren't my hands," the man complained as he tried to put his free hand in front of LaStanza's eyes. With a quick jerk, LaStanza twisted the man around and cuffed both hands him behind his back before picking up the automatic.

"They're *moon* hands!" the man cried.

On the way to Charity Hospital, the man told LaStanza he was a second generation clone. Then he started pleading for the LaStanza to take him to Tchoupitoulas and Jackson Avenue–to catch his flight–to Alpha Six.

"This one needs a ride," LaStanza told the standard-issue, heavy-set, flat-faced admitting nurse. "Put him on the nonstop to Mandeville." It was nut house time, absolutely.

"Must be a full moon tonight," the bored nurse said. "All the loonies are out."

While LaStanza was filling out his report, a Seventh District patrolman came in with a howling man.

"What's his problem?" LaStanza asked.

"He thinks the world's being taken over by clones."

LaStanza couldn't resist. "Put him in with mine. He's a second generation clone."

The patrolman eagerly obliged. LaStanza and the other cop watched the two men standing at opposite ends of the small trauma room, hissing and spitting at one another. LaStanza laughed so hard, his side ached. He'd been on the street long enough to not pass up an opportunity like that. Laughs were hard to find along the bloody streets of the Sixth District.

The Man With Moon Hands became one of LaStanza's favorite cop stories, especially after the man was released, as all nut cases inevitably were. The frizzy-haired loony began waiting every night at Tchoupitoulas and Jackson Avenue–for his flight–to Alpha Six. No matter the weather, he would be there, standing with his tattered brown suitcase in front of the old, abandoned New Orleans Cotton Exchange. No one bothered him. Most people probably figured he was just waiting in the wrong place for the Jackson Avenue Ferry.

One evening LaStanza watched The Man With Moon Hands for an hour and the man never moved a muscle. He stood patiently, the moon hands wrapped around the suitcase, the bulging eyes tilted upward at the dark sky, as he waited– for his flight–to Alpha Six.

Then LaStanza got transferred to Homicide. Three years later, LaStanza was in a different alley.

———

"What's the matter wit' you?" Snowood yelled, "I thought you was gonna canvass?"

LaStanza climbed off the cases and started down the alley. He was still looking at the body.

"Mark and I are taking Wyatt, Jr. here to the Bureau for his statement," Snowood said. To Snowood, a cop who shot someone had to be related, no matter how distantly, to Wyatt Earp, himself.

LaStanza watched as the corpse was zipped into a black body bag and hauled off by the coroner's assistants. In the span of two minutes, he was alone. But there was nothing to canvass. It was a dead end alley with no doors or windows, just brick walls and rusted dumpsters and bent-up garbage cans. It was a garbage alley.

It became very quiet. If he strained, LaStanza could hear cars in the distance, but it was silent in the alley. There was no movement except for the gnats circling over the fresh blood, and the rats crouching in anticipation of the moment when the detective would be gone.

On his way out of the alley, he remembered something else. He remembered yet another alley, back when he was a rookie. It was Mardi Gras morning and someone had killed a cop. LaStanza found the cop killer in a foggy alley. The man had a gun and it was over in less than a second. It was a good shooting, a clean shooting.

He'd shot the man without hesitation. And he wondered about that, about the intangible, about the unspoken reason a cop shoots one and not another. Maybe there was something in the moon man's frantic eyes that told LaStanza not to shoot. Maybe it was the frizzy hair. Or maybe, it was the moon white hands.

———

"Looks like a good shooting," Sergeant Mark Land told LaStanza when he arrived at the Homicide Office. "Looks like our man had no choice."

LaStanza sat heavily in his chair and didn't answer.

Big, burly and Italian, with thick dark hair and a full moustache, Mark looked like an oversized version of LaStanza. Grinning broadly, the sergeant pulled up Snowood's chair and began to run down the patrolman's statement in detail, but LaStanza wasn't listening. He was thinking about the faded bricks of the old Cotton Exchange and the rusted drain pipes and all the lonely nights spent looking up at an empty sky.

When Mark finished, he yawned and said, "Shit, we'll be outta here in no time."

LaStanza leaned back in his chair and closed his eyes, but only for a moment.

"Say boy, what's wrong wit' you?" Snowood called out as he approached. "You been acting spooky."

"It's nothing."

"Don't give me that shit. What's the matter?"

"Nothing, I told you." LaStanza scooped up his black coffee mug with its small inscription that read: FUCK THIS SHIT! He moved over to the coffee pot and poured the hot coffee-and-chicory into his mug, then filled his sergeant's cup when Mark stepped up. The young patrolman moved up with a Styrofoam cup. LaStanza put the pot down and turned away.

"Something wrong?" the patrolman quickly asked in a shaky voice.

"No," Mark answered quickly.

LaStanza turned back and looked at the patrolman, noticing how the man's hand shook when he poured the coffee.

"He pulled the same gun on me a couple years ago," LaStanza said.

"What?" Mark said as he nearly spilled his coffee.

LaStanza took in a deep breath before adding, "That was The Man With Moon Hands."

"I'll be damned!" Mark did spill his coffee this time.

Switching his cup to his other hand, Mark turned to the patrolman and said, "You killed a legend tonight, pal."

"What are y'all yakkin' about?" Snowood asked from his desk.

"Your victim was The Man With Moon Hands," Mark told him.

"No shit?"

LaStanza watched the patrolman's eyes. There was confusion in the eyes, along with a touch of fear.

"You never heard of The Man With Moon Hands?" Mark asked the patrolman.

"No," the man answered softly. "I've only been on the road six months."

"He was the most famous 103M in the city."

"At least we know who he is now," Snowood injected. "Sumbitch had no ID on him."

"He was a 103M?" the patrolman asked LaStanza, who did not respond. Turning back at Mark, the patrolman added, "He did look weird."

"What was his name?" Snowood asked his partner.

"I don't remember," LaStanza answered, still watching the patrolman, "but it's gotta be in the computer."

"Well I'll be," the patrolman sighed in relief. "He was crazy!"

LaStanza couldn't stop his voice from sounding vicious, "You couldn't see that?"

"What am I?" the patrolman snapped back, "a psychiatrist?" He seemed stunned.

LaStanza gave him the Sicilian stare, the one that went straight through to the back of the man's skull. Then he walked back to his desk and flopped in his chair.

The exasperated patrolman continued explaining to Mark, "He looked right at me and pointed the gun and zapped me." The patrolman's voice began to rise as he followed the sergeant back into the interview room. "How'd he get the gun back anyway?"

"Goddamn courts release everything now days," Mark growled angrily.

<hr>

LaStanza was finishing his daily report, when the patrolman approached. Snowood had gone to the computer to try and identify The Man With Moon Hands.

"Excuse me, Detective LaStanza. Can I have a word with you?" The patrolman looked like a dog lost out in the rain.

LaStanza nodded to his partner's empty chair.

The patrolman's voice was almost a whisper, "I didn't know he was . . . a legend."

"He was a second generation clone."

"What?"

"Forget it."

The patrolman's hands were shaking again. He looked like he wanted to run away. Gulping, he managed to say, "How was I supposed to know?"

LaStanza said nothing.

"He pointed a gun at me."

"You didn't see a tall man with thick glasses near the alley, did you?"

"No." The patrolman looked back anxiously.

LaStanza just nodded and went back to his daily.

After a minute, the whisper voice of the patrolman came back. "When he drew down on you, why didn't you shoot him?"

Get Caught Up!

Shop all the back issues of Pulphouse at...

pulphousemagazine.com

There it was again, the intangible. How do you explain what couldn't be explained? How do you explain what was incapable of even being comprehended by the mind, incapable of being distinguished by any of the senses? How do you explain something like that?

LaStanza knew he could not. You just knew.

Peering back into a pair of searching eyes, LaStanza recognized something. He recognized a look. It was a look that said, "I've got something to live with for the rest of my life." He'd seen that same look in his own mirror.

"I passed the shoot-don't-shoot class with an 'A' at the academy," the patrolman said in a strained voice.

"Some things can't be taught," LaStanza said, finally. "Some things can't even be explained. You just know."

"You didn't shoot him and I did," the patrolman said. "Why?"

"I just knew."

It was as if he'd reached over and slapped the patrolman across the face. It took a second for the man to recover. He looked away from LaStanza's eyes and took in a couple breaths before asking, "Do you think I'll have any trouble with the Grand Jury?"

"Don't worry about it," LaStanza heard himself say. "It was a good shooting."

ANNIE REED

Professional writer Annie Reed writes stories that span genres and are always powerful. In fact with Annie, you just never know the type of story you might be reading, but you will always know it will grab you and be a compelling read.

So far Annie has had a story in every issue of this magazine and as the editor, I hope to continue that streak.

Annie's stories have appeared in four Best Mystery Stories of the Year *volumes so far. Look for so much more of Annie's work at her website* anniereed.wordpress.com.

THE PROMISE

ANNIE REED

Russell turned up the collar of his overcoat against a stiff November wind blowing from the north. The overcast sky was threatening rain. It might turn to snow if the temperatures dropped low enough overnight, or settle on that mix of rain and snow that made walking an exercise in squelching through half-frozen slush seasoned with car exhaust and grit.

The text he'd received that morning from Malachai said to meet him at three on the corner of Hightower and Seventh Avenue. Russell might have blown off the meeting if he'd been awake when the text came in, or if the request had come from anybody else.

Russell was still on nights, one of three detectives—not counting his soon-to-be-retired partner Vic Damonte—who rotated in and out of the night shift. When they were on night duty, he hit the sheets every morning about the same time most of the city was heading to work. Three in the afternoon was right in the middle of breakfast.

Russell had grown used to the late hours. The precinct was usually pretty quiet at night, and it wasn't like he had anyone at home waiting for him.

But this was Malachi Rosen. He hadn't heard from Malachi in years.

Fourteen years ago Malachi's only child had been found beaten to death and stuffed behind a pile of black plastic trash bags full of donated clothes at the base of a donation bin in the alley behind the Catholic church on Seventh Avenue.

Malachi wanted to meet across the street from that church. That wasn't a coincidence. With Malachi, nothing was ever a coincidence.

In the years since Russell had earned his gold shield, a handful of homicide cases had gone unsolved. Each of those murders haunted him, but Malachi's daughter Rachel had been the worst.

Russell had been young and stupid and his detective's shield had still been shiny bright when he and the first detective he'd been partnered with had caught the Rosen case. Russell had made a stupid mistake. Said the wrong thing, something he'd never say now, no matter how devastated a homicide victim's family was. No matter how much they begged.

He'd promised Rachel's parents that he'd catch her killer.

He'd promised Malachi and his wife that their daughter would get justice, but the police hadn't kept that promise.

Russell hadn't kept his promise.

Not for a lack of trying. He'd worked the case night and

day. Took the file home with him. Haunted the murder site. Pestered the lab techs. Canvassed and recanvassed the neighborhood.

All of it came to nothing. He'd never even come up with a viable suspect.

And now Malachi wanted to meet with him.

Russell had let dispatch know he had a meeting with a witness. It was only a little white lie—Malachi wasn't a witness—but it wasn't the first lie Russell had told in all the years he'd been a detective, and it wouldn't be the last.

Besides, Malachi might actually have something worthwhile to tell him. And if he didn't? If he just wanted to stand in the cold November afternoon and talk?

Russell would oblige.

He owed the old man that much.

———

Back when he'd been married, back when his wife had been healthy and cancer wasn't a part of their lives, Russell had worked the occasional night shift. He'd come home in the morning to the smell of pot roast or oven-roasted chicken, and they'd sit at their small kitchen table and eat dinner while the sun came up over the city.

Those were the days when most people could afford to put beef on the table a few days a week, even on a beat cop's salary. After dinner, Russell would stumble off to bed and his wife would go to work at a department store, and when he got up in the middle of the afternoon, he'd make himself breakfast. Scrambled eggs and toast. And bacon if he didn't oversleep and his wife had put in extra hours at the store.

His wife had been gone for years now. When he got home after work, dinner was something he could throw in the microwave while he was in the shower. But he'd kept up the habit of cooking himself breakfast, the same breakfast he'd eaten day after day.

Vic told him all those eggs would kill him someday. Screw with his cholesterol. Vic had suffered a minor heart attack a couple of years back. He hadn't turned into a health food nut after that—he snuck in a donut or a bagel with cream cheese every now and then—but he enjoyed spreading the misery of a low fat, low carb lifestyle. Russell was a favorite target.

Vic might be right, but breakfast was part of Russell's routine. A piece of his married life he could hang onto like the framed snapshots of his wife he kept in his bedroom. If he knew how to cook pot roast like his wife had cooked it, he'd probably make that for himself every now and then too. Cooking eggs in the same frying pan his wife had used made the apartment smell, at least a little bit, like it used to when she was still alive.

Made the empty place smell like home.

This afternoon Russell broke his routine so he could get out the door in time for his meeting with Malachi. He'd stopped at a fast food joint that served breakfast 24/7. He'd picked up a large coffee and a breakfast burrito that looked halfway decent on the menu board but proved to be disappointing in person. He'd thrown most of it in a trash bin he passed as he walked the few blocks up Seventh Avenue toward Hightower from the parking garage where he'd left his car.

At least the coffee was good. There was enough still left in the cardboard go cup to warm his hands. On a day like today, that was a plus.

Only a handful of people were out on the street. Not surprising. The parking garage was attached to a busy medical center. A pedestrian walkway connected the second floor of the garage to the medical center. Great for patients and the doctors and nurses and other staff who parked in the garage, especially on cold November days, but hell on local businesses who depended on foot traffic.

The closer Russell got to Hightower, the more the neighborhood changed from healthcare providers to a mix of small, independent businesses housed in buildings that had been built fifty years before the turn of the century. A CPA occupied the ground floor of a three-story walkup next to a beauty salon. Small apartments took up the second and third stories. A small discount clothing store, its storefront already decorated for the holiday season, shared the ground floor of another three-story building with a liquor store, an Asian grocer, and a Greek deli.

Stunted oaks, their bare branches rattling in the wind, lined Seventh Avenue on both sides, standing sentry in their caged planters every ten feet or so.

The trees had been planted a decade earlier, a low-cost concession by the city to entice the medical center's investors to build in the neighborhood. Electrical outlets had been installed near the base of each tree. In another week or so city workers would be decorating the trees with hundreds of twinkle lights.

The medical center was supposed to be a boon for the neighborhood. That's how the city had sold the idea to the existing businesses. And for some it had been a boon. The liquor store stayed open 24/7 now, and the Greek deli had extended its hours. Russell doubted the beauty salon or the discount clothing store had done as well. Some of the older homes in the area had been converted to doctors' offices, and while the former residents of those homes might take a walk to get their hair done or pick up a new outfit, the doctors and staffs in those refurbished homes rarely did.

After a few years, the local merchants had had enough. If the medical center could get concessions from the city, they figured they could too. They fought for any sort of improvements that would draw people into their stores.

The city planners took a look at the neighborhood and figured they were sitting on a gold mine. The older buildings brought in tax dollars, but newer buildings, taller buildings, modern commercial buildings, could bring in so much more.

So began the renovation of the neighborhood. Some of the oldest and most outdated buildings were torn down, to be replaced with shiny new multi-use, multi-story complexes. The fact that those demolitions would displace residents and current businesses was just the cost of progress. The building that used to house a collectibles store and a new-and-used bookstore was gone now. In its place, a new high rise condominium was taking shape behind a boarded-up section of sidewalk.

Russell wondered how many more of the buildings housing current businesses and residences would be gone in the next couple of years. If the current residents had wished they'd kept their mouths shut instead of pestering the politicians to improve their neighborhood. The new buildings would attract people, that was certain, but would any of the old merchants still be here?

As far as Russell was concerned, the whole mess was a prime example of "be careful what you wish for."

As he got closer to the intersection at Hightower, he realized why Malachi wanted to meet him in this particular place. Telltale orange cones and construction signs blocked part of the street in front of the church.

Or what was left of the church.

A bulldozer was busy tearing down the old brick-front Catholic church and the multipurpose hall attached to it. All that was left of the church was a portion of the front wall and the concrete steps leading up from the sidewalk to the entryway. A brick alcove facing Seventh Avenue was still standing, almost like it was protecting the statue of the Virgin Mary still standing inside. The multipurpose hall had been reduced to a pile of rubble.

Malachai was standing on the sidewalk on the other side of Seventh Avenue, almost directly across the street from that statue, his back toward Russell. The old man had on a brown fedora, a tan overcoat, and a black scarf wrapped around his neck.

Russell didn't call out a greeting. Between the sound of the on-going demolition and city traffic, the old man would never hear him.

"I'd offer you some coffee," Russell said in lieu of hello when he reached Malachi, "but if I remember right, you don't drink the stuff."

Malachai grunted. "Never picked up the habit."

He didn't turn to look at Russell.

"Probably better off." Russell hunched his shoulders

against the cold and nodded at the half-demolished building. "Didn't realize they were tearing this place down."

If the case had still been active, he would have known. Maybe he should have known anyway, should have paid attention to the renovations going on in the neighborhood in more than just the casual way someone does who reads the local news online over breakfast. But who would have thought the church would be among the buildings scheduled to be replaced?

"The developer offered the diocese a bucketload of money," Malachi said.

He turned his head to give Russell a sideways glance. Russell was shocked to see how old—how really *old*—Malachi looked. His chin and cheeks sported sparse white stubble, and the skin beneath looked sallow. The blue of his eyes behind wire-rim glasses had faded, the whites more ivory than white and shot through with tiny red veins.

He didn't just look old. He looked sick.

"They even kicked in some land for the diocese to build a new church complex," Malachi said. "Or so I heard."

That sideways glance held Russell's for a long moment before Malachi turned back to look at the destruction going on across the street.

The glance said *Why don't you know all this? Why did I have to tell you?*

The glance said *You'd have known if you still looking for the bastard who killed my Rachel.*

The glance said *You broke your promise.*

Or maybe that was just Russell's guilt talking. You'd think after all this time, the guilt would have faded away.

But time, that old sonofabitch, had only made it worse.

———

A city bus swept past them, fouling the air with the diesel smoke left in its wake. Some of the buses in the city had been refitted to burn cleaner fuel, or at least the kind you couldn't see polluting the air. This wasn't one of them.

Russell took a sip of his coffee and grimaced. It was getting cold, and the cold made it taste bitter. He thought about throwing what was left in the trash receptacle halfway up the block, but he didn't want to walk away from Malachi and the old man didn't look like he intended to move from his spot anytime soon.

"Maryann used to keep in touch with some of the women in the church group," Malachi said. "Those old birds love gossip more than they love Jesus. I think that's one of the reasons she didn't…"

He shrugged but didn't finish the sentence. He didn't need to. Russell caught his meaning.

Maryann was Malachi's wife. She was also a devout Catholic who'd been a member of the congregation of the church currently being reduced to rubble. Her daughter's murder hadn't been enough to make her question her faith or her devotion to this particular parish.

"She doesn't talk to them anymore?"

"She passed away in April," Malachi said. "Cancer."

Seven months ago. Russell hadn't known that either. From the looks of her husband, Maryann might not have been the only one touched by cancer.

"I'm sorry to hear that," Russell said.

Malachi shrugged again. "It was quick. A mercy, the priest said. She didn't suffer, he said. As if he knew what suffering was."

The words were bitter, but the old man's voice was eerily neutral, like he was discussing the weather with a stranger on the bus. It was probably Malachi's way of working up to whatever he wanted to say.

Fourteen years ago, Malachi had been much more direct. He'd called the precinct every day, always asking for Russell, never Russell's partner. Malachi's questions were always the same. *Any news? Any leads?* So was Russell's answer. *We're working on it. We'll let you know when we get something.*

But they never had.

The department didn't have the money for all the high-tech stuff everyone saw on TV, even back then. Resources had to be budgeted. If it had been more than one little girl, Russell and his partner might have been able to convince the department to do the kind of analysis the general public assumed was done on every case. Samples had been collected, of course. Hair and fiber and other trace evidence. Photographs taken. All kept on file for comparison to whoever they hauled in for questioning.

There'd been no blood splatter at the scene. Malachi's daughter had been killed elsewhere and transported to church property. That meant something important to her killer. What, they'd never figured out.

Russell's partner at the time had had his theories. The little girl hadn't been sexually assaulted and there was no semen mixed in with the blood on her or her clothes, so the killer wasn't a garden variety pedophile. She'd been beaten with a blunt object, something like a baseball bat, but it had to be an aluminum bat since there'd been no wood fibers in the wounds. She hadn't been strangled. She was still wearing the clothes she'd left home with that morning before she went to school.

The first blow to the back of her head had caved her skull in and killed her outright. A blessing considering that her killer had kept hitting her until the bones in her arms and legs and most of her ribs had been broken. The autopsy had confirmed those blows had been post-mortem.

Whoever had killed her had been angry. Furious. A beating like that came from rage.

There'd been no usable fingerprints found on her body or her backpack, which had been left next to the body. The alley behind the church was paved, and no useful tire tracks had been noted on the asphalt. No one in the neighborhood had seen anyone driving into or leaving the alley.

They'd investigated Malachi's family as a matter of course. He'd told the police he had no enemies, a sentiment shared by the people who knew him. Rachel had the normal amount of run-ins with the popular girls at school. Mean girls, as they'd been known back in Russell's public school days, and some of them had been more than simply mean. But that avenue of the investigation led nowhere.

They'd widened the investigation to include anyone who'd threatened the church. The priest. The nuns or any of the catechism teachers. Russell's partner thought Rachel might have been a convenient substitute for whoever the killer really wanted to murder. A lot of people back then had been angry at priests, all Catholic priests, but the pastor at this church seemed universally well liked.

The more people they looked at, the more nothing they turned up.

All they had was Rachel's body and her backpack. With no leads, eventually the case had been backburnered. Russell abhorred that part of police work, but all he could do about it was to continue working the case on his time off.

"She was only twelve," Malachi said now. "Twelve. She'd be twenty-six. Today." He sniffed but his cheeks were dry. "It's her birthday."

Russell didn't know what to say to that, so he kept his mouth shut. He hadn't realized that today was Rachel's birthday. He'd committed so many facts about her murder to memory, but her birthday hadn't been one of them.

Fair-haired Rachel had been the Rosens' late-in-life child. They had no other children and had given up trying years before. When they found they were going to have a baby, they'd called her a gift from God.

Malachi was Jewish, but his wife had insisted that their

child be raised in her religion. It was a big thing for Catholics that any children be raised in the faith. Russell's own mother had done the same thing, raising him Catholic. Malachi loved his wife more than his own faith, and so Rachel had been baptized in the church that was now little more than rubble and memories.

A month into the investigation, when it must have become clear to the Rosens that the police might not ever find Rachel's killer, Maryann Rosen had brought an old-fashioned picture album full of photographs of Rachel to the precinct. Pictures of baby Rachel taking her first steps. Staring in wonder at her first Christmas tree. Chasing after the Rosens' dog in their backyard. Rachel in her frilly white first communion dress, her proud parents standing behind her.

Russell never asked if Malachi had witnessed his daughter's first communion. Malachi had told him once that he wasn't a practicing Jew, but he never mentioned if he went to Mass with his wife.

"I keep God in my own way," he'd said once. "For a Jew who fell in love with a Catholic woman, I always believed God would understand."

Russell hadn't given the remark much thought at the time. Russell kept God in his own way, too. His own mother had been devout, and he'd kept going to Mass as an adult more out of habit than anything else. That stopped after his wife died and Russell found he no longer had the stomach for the religious rituals his mother had put so much faith in.

Now, though? As he stood next to the man who looked like age had finally caught up with him, Russell wondered if Malachi had ever lost his faith in God after his daughter's murder. Or if he'd lost his faith when the police hadn't been able to find her killer, much less bring him to justice.

The last and best theory Russell and his partner had was that whoever had killed Rachel must have spotted her leaving her catechism class the afternoon she'd been murdered. Classes were held in the church's multipurpose building, and witnesses—including the nun who'd taught the class—said Rachel had left on time for the walk home.

Somewhere in the mile between the church and the Rosens' home, Rachel's killer had snatched her off the street.

A crime of opportunity.

And a killer they'd never caught.

Rachel Rosen's murder had been the first homicide Russell had worked, long before he'd been partnered with Vic Damonte. His partner at the time had been a veteran detective who put up with exactly zero bullshit from a cop still learning the difference between being a beat cop and a detective.

Russell had been gung-ho and full of himself. He'd gone with his partner to do the notification to family. He'd watched Maryann Rosen collapse in the doorway of their home. Seen the blood drain from Malachi's face as the finality of what Russell's partner told them sank in.

Their daughter was dead.

Up until then, she'd simply been late getting home from catechism. The Rosens had called all her friends, all her friends' friends. All the catechism teachers and the women in

Maryann's church group. Their friends had combed the neighborhood, gone to the stores where the kids sometimes hung out after school, went to stores where none of the kids hung out, all looking for Rachel while her parents waited anxiously at home.

Rachel's name was on the backpack found next to her body. On the school books inside her backpack. On her catechism books. The pastor at the church had given the police her address, and Russell and his partner had gone to the Rosens' home to notify her parents.

It had been Russell's first notification visit, and he'd made a serious mistake. He'd promised the Rosens that he'd catch their daughter's killer.

It was the first and last time he'd ever made a promise like that.

His partner had gone ballistic.

"You don't make a fucking promise you can't keep," he'd said. "You're not doing the family any favors. It'll eat you up inside, and they'll come to hate you for breaking your promise."

Russell had taken the rebuke as a personal insult. "How do you know we won't find the guy?"

He'd thought about saying that *he'd* find the guy. At least he'd been smart enough to keep that thought to himself.

"Because, smart guy," his partner had said, "unless the killer's as dumb as a doornail or makes a mistake somewhere down the line, or somebody has a beef with him and gives him up, it's 50/50 if we catch him or not."

His partner had gone on to cite manpower, caseload, the

city's transient and homeless population, all the whack jobs on the street thanks to cutbacks in mental health services.

"We got too much on our plate as is," he'd said. "This case'll catch some media attention because it's a kid, so we might get a few extra days to work it, but then somebody's gonna shoot somebody else or a lot of somebody elses, and we'll have to backburner this one."

Which was exactly what happened.

The case kept getting backburnered again and again. Russell took the casefile home, poured over the details while his wife was at work, followed up leads and reinterviewed witnesses as time allowed, but the case kept getting colder and colder.

When Malachi texted Russell that morning and asked for the meeting, Russell realized he hadn't looked at the file in years.

He felt guilty about that, too.

———

"My liver's failing," Malachi said.

Across the street, the alcove holding the Virgin Mary's statue was reduced to a pile of bricks under a fresh assault from a bulldozer with a bucket bigger than Russell's car. The statue remained standing.

"I caught your expression when you looked at me," Malachi continued. "That look of shock you tried to cover up. I get that from people who haven't seen me in a while. 'You got old.' I hear that one a lot." He gave Russell a sideways glance again. "You shouldn't play poker with that face."

Russell shouldn't have been surprised. One look at Malachi's face had told him something was wrong, but Russell still felt a pang of sadness he hadn't expected.

He debated taking another sip of coffee, decided against it. "I'll keep that in mind," he said. "You getting treated for that?"

Malachi shrugged. "They tell me I need a new liver. I tell them give it to someone's got a life in front of them. Me? I think I've been around long enough."

Russell didn't know much about liver failure. He seemed to recall liver failure and alcoholism went hand in hand, but Malachi'd never struck him as someone who drank to excess. He certainly didn't look drunk now.

"That why you set up this meeting?" Russell asked. "You wanted to tell me you don't have much time left?"

Not much time for Russell to keep his promise before it was forever too late.

"Nope."

Across the street, the statue of the Virgin Mary joined the pile of brick rubble. Russell wondered why the church hadn't removed the statue, preserved it somehow. His mother would have been scandalized.

"I'm here to let you off the hook," Malachi said. "I took care of it for you."

He said that last part so quietly that Russell almost missed what he said thanks to the strident backup beeps from the bulldozer and a reverberating bass beat from a passing car on Seventh Avenue.

When the words sunk in, Russell turned to look Malachi full in the face. This time Russell didn't try to hide his shock.

"What do you mean, 'took care of it'?" he asked.

Another city bus went by, belching diesel smoke. The side of the bus was plastered with one of those wraparound ads for a chain store in the new mall south of town.

"A little over a year ago, I started getting these notes on my car," Malachi said. "Under the windshield wipers. Mostly bible verses. Didn't think much of it at the time." He shrugged. "Lots of crazies in the world today, but I don't have to tell you that."

A small ball of tension was settling in Russell's belly that had nothing to do with the few bites of the burrito he'd had for breakfast or the cold coffee he still held in one hand.

"Then Maryann got sick and the notes stopped for a while. To tell the truth, I didn't even notice."

Malachi shoved his hands into the pockets of his overcoat. His eyes had taken on a faraway look, like he was living in his memories, not standing on a city street across from where they'd found his daughter's body.

"They started again after she died," Malachi said. "Did I tell you she wanted a funeral Mass? I hadn't set foot in church since the day you came to tell me our Rachel was gone, but I honored her wishes. She got her funeral Mass." He nodded across the street. "In that church. It was a nice service. They got a new priest. He made an effort." Malachi's shoulders hunched as he took a deep breath. "I got the first threat the next day."

"You report this?" Russell asked. If Malachi had, no one had ever told him.

Malachi shot him a look. "So you could do what? Fill out another report that goes nowhere?"

There was a great deal of anger now in the old man's faded eyes. Russell had earned that anger, so he kept his mouth shut.

Traffic was getting heavier as the day wound down to rush hour. Russell stepped closer to Malachi so he wouldn't miss anything the old man said.

"I started writing back," Malachi said. "What else did I have to keep myself busy? I hear people do this on the Internet, argue with the crazies. This was like that in real life. I left little notes under my own windshield wipers before I went to bed. They were always gone in the morning."

Russell couldn't keep quiet any more. "Do you have any idea how dangerous that is? This whack job knows where you live."

The world was full of fanatics who believed the world would be better off without whatever group was the current target of their hate. Jews had always been high on that list.

Malachi shrugged. "The world has always been a dangerous place. I shouldn't have to tell you that."

He pulled a piece of paper out of his pocket and held it out to Russell.

Russell reached out to take it, but Malachi held on for a moment too long, and Russell thought the old man had changed his mind.

"Don't forget us," he said, and he let go of the note.

Then he stepped off the curb and into traffic.

Russell grabbed for him but managed only to brush Malachi's overcoat with his fingers.

The first two cars swerved and missed the old man.

The city bus didn't.

———

They found a body right where Malachi's note said it would be.

Buried in a shallow grave in an empty lot east of town. Not the empty lot the developer had purchased as the site for the new church facility—even Malachi in his pain and his rage wouldn't have been that sacrilegious—but the site of a housing development that had gone bankrupt before the model homes were even built.

Malachi hadn't known the man's name, or if he had, he didn't include it in the note. The only thing in the shallow grave besides the body was a handgun, a little .22 pistol. Malachi's prints were on the gun as well as the bullets.

The coroner estimated that the man had been dead for at least four months. Cause of death was a single gunshot wound to the back of his head, almost in the same place where Rachel's killer had struck her with a baseball bat. The little .22 pistol had done its job.

The coroner also found marks on the body that indicated the man had been hit with a taser. The dead man was decades younger than Malachi. The taser charge explained how Malachi was able to subdue him.

The dead man's hair matched hair taken from Rachel's body. It tied him to Rachel, but would it have been enough to convict him in a court of law? Probably not, but it had been enough for Malachi. Maybe the man had even bragged about it. Russell wouldn't have put it past him. His prints were on file from when he'd been arrested at a protest outside a Jewish synagogue that had turned violent. He was forty-one years old, which meant he'd been twenty-seven when Rachel had been murdered.

Had he snatched Rachel deliberately because she'd been the child of a Jewish father? Or had the murder been a crime of opportunity as Russell's partner at the time had believed?

They'd never know. If the man had told Malachi before he'd died, that information had died along with Malachi the day the old man stepped into the middle of rush hour traffic.

Vic Damonte refused to have anything to do with wrapping up the case. "We got enough on our plate," he told Russell. "This is your albatross, you deal with it."

That was fine with Russell.

He filed reports as they came in, crossed all the Ts and dotted the Is, and when he was done, he was finally able to cross Rachel's murder off the unsolved list.

Had justice finally been done?

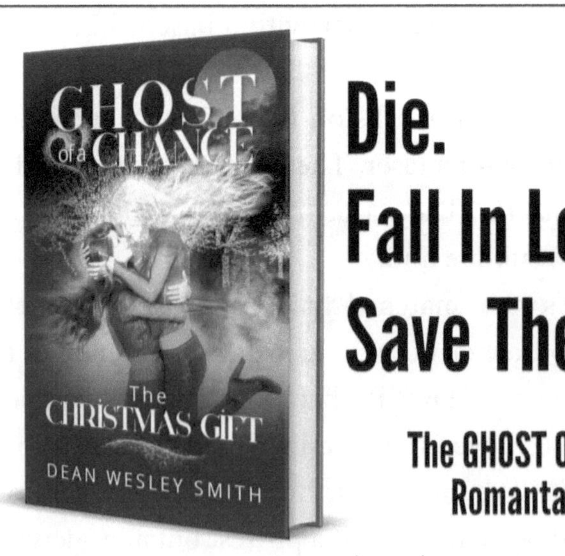

He didn't know. Three more people were dead—Malachi and his wife, and a racist who'd believed Jewish people were less than human. A man who harbored hatred in his heart even as he hit his knees in church every Sunday and professed his love of god in the same church where Malachi had held the funeral for his wife.

The last piece of evidence that Russell put in Rachel's casefile was the note that Malachi had given him. The note that explained what he did and where the police could find the body. It was part of the evidence of the case, not that anyone would ever open this file again. The case was over, at least officially.

Unofficially?

Russell's old partner had been right. This case would haunt him for the rest of his life. Not only because he'd made a promise he couldn't keep. A promise to a dead child and her grieving family that her killer would be brought to justice.

No, what would really haunt Russell was the look in Malachi's eyes right before he stepped off the curb. A look of such profound sadness that it made Russell's jaded heart break.

Especially when he read the last line Malachi had written on the piece of paper he'd handed to Russell.

I made a promise to her too.

ROB VAGLE

Rob Vagle is a veteran short story writer who is becoming a regular contributor to these pages, something I am very happy about. I feel lucky to have his work here. And you will understand that after reading this fantastic ghost story. But it is not really a ghost story, more of a love story. And an afterlife story. And a science fiction story. Typical Rob story, impossible to put into a simple description.

But it is wonderfully powerful.

I suggest you go to robvagle.com to find out a lot more about his fantastic stories and books.

CLOSING TIME

ROB VAGLE

The back door of the bar was a double door, twelve feet high, and made of an ancient wood that looked like it would give you splinters if you touched it. Adam touched it once. Placed the palm of his hand against it, pressed it against the surprisingly cold and the not so surprisingly hard wood. It had felt gritty and dusty, and he felt sharp pricks on his skin. He thought he had gotten splinters and when he removed his hand and inspected every finger and the palm, he found nothing. No dust, no grit, and no splinters. Yet his hand tingled, needles and pins, fading a moment later.

Those double doors had large iron rings to pull the doors open. Adam had never tried to touch the rings, let alone pull on them. If he opened the door, even accidentally, he'd have to walk though and go to the other side. Whatever was there on the other side, life after death.

Instead, he waited for Margaret.

For ninety years he waited for her.

Adam watched the Korean couple go out the double doors with longing and a healthy kick of envy because Jae-Lee, a hotel owner from Seoul, South Korea, died in an airplane crash and had waited in this place for twenty years for Soon-Bok to show up.

They held hands (of course) and stepped into the gray looming like fog outside. They turned to shadows, their shadows turning into liquid and the fog soaked them up like a sponge soaks up water. As the double doors closed, he caught the sight of their shadows streaming into rivulets, branching out, spreading out to somewhere. Then the doors closed and he was in the dark again.

Because of waiting.

"You have that look on your face again," the bartender said.

Fafa was her name, whatever kind of name that was—she always said it was a name older than time. She'd been watching him and now she rested her forearms on the bar, her sleeves rolled up past the elbows. Her hair was silver and shoulder length. There was an elegance to her and Adam thought she seemed too classy even for a joint so close to what many other people called the perpetual light. She reminded him of Lauren Bacall in her senior years, like the way she looked in the movie Misery he'd seen a few years before his death.

She smelled like cloves whenever she was near and Adam should have known she was there. He would have spun around on the stool and stagger away so that he wouldn't have to hear the same old thing he was destined to hear for eternity if he'd never step through those double doors. Whenever he made eye contact with her and was besieged by those deep green eyes, he froze into place, riveted under her consideration.

"You have options," she said and the corner of her lips turned up in a smile. She winked as if they shared a secret, which in fact it was a simple eternal script. "You can leave here. Right through those same doors."

It wasn't uncomfortable looking into her eyes, and her eyes looking into his. He thought he had a physical heart again and not just an illusion of one. She perked him right up like he was alive again. On Earth. With Margaret and the two of them rolling around on the bed together in their old Victorian house in San Francisco.

He wondered, if he felt alive whenever he looked into Fafa's eyes why did he feel like stepping into that fog he saw the Korean couple walk into? That didn't look like life—it definitely looked like death. Life was through the front door, the same door everyone entered. The senses, flesh and blood. The back door, those double doors? He didn't know what was out there. The front door, now there he knew what he'd left behind.

"Where is she?" he asked Fafa. "It's been ninety years. She's one hundred and twenty years old now."

"You have the other option," Fafa said.

On the top shelf behind her, the black bottles glittered. Those bottles held nightmares, horrid memories, and pain. Things of war, disease, human suffering perpetrated by human evil. Among those bottles, there was one drink, Fafa had told him, that would allow him to go back to the living. The transformation upon drinking it would send him back as a ghost. He'd be something that moved through walls. Fafa assured him he'd be able to communicate with Margaret upon moving his ghostly hand through her living flesh. He was tethered to her. She was the reason why he waited.

Fafa also emphasized the change. He wouldn't be the same when he returned, whether with her or without her.

"What's the harm in the wait? Wait for as long as you have to," Fafa said. "You've waited this long."

A switch was flicked inside his mind and she could see it. Fafa was a good therapist, Adam thought. Or the ultimate bartender—isn't that why drinkers poured their souls out to one? She presented him with his options in that calming, unassuming way of hers. With observation, she played off his moods and changed direction, like now, with the reminder of the black bottle and the silent question: *or are you ready for that drink?*

Her behavior used to irk Adam when he first came here. She'd change her mind and say something opposite that he'd think she was hiding something from him. If he'd learned one thing in this place that never changed in ninety years, it was Fafa wasn't hiding anything. Perhaps she knew everything.

About life. About the universe. Free will, to her, was paramount, and she reminded every patron in here.

"I might need a drink from that bottle soon," he said. Again, he wondered how the hell do you measure days in here.

She crossed her arms and brought her hand up to touch her chin, considering him. Her green eyes glowed like sunlight though leaves in a tree.

"Is it now, Adam?"

———

Fafa said this place had no name, so Adam called it The Eternal Bar. He entered through the front door, which wasn't as impressive as the double-door in the back. The front door was a single, also made of wood, but he never touched it because the door swung open to allow him to enter. That's the way everyone entered this place. The door would swing open as if great guest of wind blew the door in.

He died in a traffic accident in 1994. He'd been a dentist and made good money probing into peoples' mouths. His parents had taught him good dental hygiene was the gateway to health, in that how he treated his own teeth affected other functions of the body, like digestion predominately. So he brushed and flossed every day and had regular check ups. A career in dentistry came naturally.

Adam didn't believe in a heaven or a hell. He certainly didn't expect to find a bar on the other side. He wasn't much of a drinker. He enjoyed a glass of red wine—a Shiraz, his favorite—from time to time and enjoyed sampling various brewpubs, having one pint of an IPA or an Amber, sure. The point was, he drank only one glass or pint. Alcohol, he could take it or leave it, and didn't miss it when he didn't have it.

So to find himself inside a bar after death was puzzling. When the front door slammed shut behind him, he just stood there. He realized how much life—no matter what your beliefs or religious affiliation—prepared you to expect a tunnel of light and friends and relatives as the bare minimum. To be thrust into a bar, was not only puzzling, but disappointing.

Whispers of conversations fluttered around him. A bright orb of light floated above him and they were scattered throughout the place. He couldn't see anything above the orbs that might support them. They were like miniature suns never winking out of existence.

He stood on a hard wood floor and straight ahead the massive bar made of polished cherry oak and brass foot railings. The stools, polished chrome and leather upholstered, lined the front. Adam had to squint at the light glowing behind the bar. It was like sunlight igniting the colors of the many rows of bottles at the back of the bar. Adam thought of Roy G Biv, and indeed the rows of bottles were organized by the color spectrum. Red on the first bottom row, orange next up, then yellow, green, blue, indigo, and violet. There was one more row. The top row, all the bottles were black like portals into the dark night.

Cigarette smoke lingered in the bar, tendrils rolling across the room. Adam couldn't remember the last time he entered a place that allowed smoking indoors. Usually he choked on the smell. Not here. The smoke didn't give him a physical reaction. He could smell it, however. It was earthy, like wet leaves. He smelled cloves—although he didn't know yet the smell emanated from Fafa.

The air in the place was neither hot nor cold. It was the way Goldie Locks liked it. The thermostat was just right.

There were people inside the bar, he could feel eyes on him from the shadows. There were tables around the room, round with no tablecloths. There were booths along the walls and he saw shadows sitting inside there. It was as if the light orbs suspended above lit areas to walk. Barely any light caressed the people lingering at the tables.

Looking past the corner of the great bar to the wall at the back, the tall double doors loomed over Adam even as he stood on the other side of the room.

"Pass through if you like." Fafa stood behind the bar, in front of the rainbow rows of bottles. "Behind those doors is the great beyond. If you're not ready, or if you'd like to wait for someone, this is the place to do it. Have a drink. Wait. Until it's time."

Her gaze drew him closer to the bar. When he touched the edge of the bar he didn't hesitate to slide onto a stool. The smell of cloves were so much stronger in front of her. He didn't feel disoriented and lost while under her attention. It was then he thought about Margaret and waiting for her. They'd been married for five years, no children, with no plans of having any. He was straight and Margaret was bi, but her more stable relationships had been with men. In time she certainly would meet someone, regardless of gender. He couldn't fault her for living. She was going back to school, perhaps to medical school. He wondered if she'd become a doctor.

"What do you have?" he asked the bartender, who had such a calming presence, he could wait a long, long time for Margaret.

She smiled and waved her hands at the rows of bottles. "We have drinks to make you remember. We have drinks to make you forget. We also have drinks to bring back a mood from any moment in your life."

From that moment on, Adam rediscovered his life. A drink from any one of the colored bottles sent him away into the shadows of the bar where he remembered and relived. The drinks were like sleep and he knew he went away for a time. He was never sure how long he was in a state of sweet hibernation. Sometimes Fafa would tell him when he talked to her at the bar. New arrivals who entered the bar tended to rouse up the whole joint. From those new arrivals, Adam could get a report of how much time had passed on Earth.

Other times he talked with the other patrons, although it was rare more than a few were awake at any one time.

He found drinks where he could remember his birth and his first few years of life in Grants Pass, Oregon. He remembered vacations on the coast and running his toes through beach sand for the first time.

The bar was a funny place. You got your social contact by drinking and remembering and reliving. Rarely did you talk to others in the bar. It was as if socializing with others in this waiting place was secondary to the reliving.

There were drinks where he relived love, and love in all its forms, from parental love to romantic love. There were drinks where he'd remember various pets in his life, like feeling the love for Baxter, the Scottish Terrier he played with when he was in elementary school.

People from his life passed through the bar. Some even knew Margaret and they told him about her. She was doing well, finished college went to medical school. No, she didn't marry again.

Then the disturbing news from Margaret's younger sister, Megan, who died at the age of sixty-two: "Margaret's not aging," she told him.

———

"I want that drink," Adam told Fafa. "Today is the day." And he felt confident about that decision.

The shot glass thumped against the oak bar top. Fafa filled the glass, the liquid clear and colorless from the black bottle. He lifted the glass and knocked his head back as the glass reached his lips. The liquid burned across his tongue and down his throat.

The bar turned white and fuzzy around the edges, until it faded to black. The shot glass dropped from his hand and bounced on the bar.

He was lost to oblivion.

When he came to, he was on Earth again. Panting and moans filled a darkened room.

He stood over a bed with a wrought iron headboard. Two figures writhed underneath a thick comforter, the moaning louder and more urgent. Both voices belonged to women. Adam knew the sound of his wife's pleasure, and knew she was under there. Being with another woman (let alone another lover) didn't surprise him. He would have expected nothing else. She was older than most people and still having sex—that surprised him.

After a shuddering gasp, Margaret's head slid out from under the comforter as she sat up, gathering up the pillows behind her back. Her hair was still dark and the bedside light caught the copper highlights. She didn't have any gray hair. Her face was tanned and although there were crow's feet at the corners of her eyes, the rest of her skin looked smooth and beautiful. Her stomach was still taut, her muscles still toned. She looked like she'd barely aged.

Disoriented, he looked around the room, for a clue about the date. Since he died, time was a hard thing to keep track of. There was a monitor on the wall, a flat, large screen. It was blank and if it was a television it was unlike one Adam had ever seen.

"Prepare the shower," Margaret said.

She said it the room as she leaned back, catching her breath, her chest rising. A door slid open on the wall, revealing a tiled room bright with light. Water splattered and fell, sounding like rain.

Margaret's lover—red hair and looked considerably younger—snuggled up to Margaret's side and curled in a fetal position. She closed her eyes with a smile on her face.

"Don't wait too long to call me again," the lover said.

Margaret patted the lover's hip and slipped out of bed.

Adam followed her into the bathroom.

The door slid shut, cutting right through him. The bathroom was already filled with steam, the mirror over the counter slick with moisture.

Margaret slid the shower door back and Adam reached out, his hand passing through her shoulder. In that instant, she saw him. She froze, her mouth pursed in a frown. Her eyes widened into a surprise.

"Adam," she whispered. Then quickly, she blurted, "Water off."

The water falling in the shower stopped.

"What happened to you?" he asked. "You're still young."

Her eye glistened with brimming tears. "I've been waiting to see you."

"So have I," he said.

He shook his head because she didn't look surprised to see his ghost.

"That's right," she said, "I knew you'd come. I've been having dreams about you. A lot. Lately. That hasn't happened since I first started taking the treatments."

"Treatments?"

"For longevity." She shook her head and tried to touch him, but her hands waved right through him. She rolled her eyes and said, "You weren't there. You remember I wanted to go back to school? Human biology. That led to medical school, which led to a program involving human longevity. The fountain of youth, Adam. Can you believe it?"

He had wanted to grow old with her. Now, he felt jealousy. He felt left behind. She had been living. He'd been waiting. Anger stirred in him.

"I've been waiting for you," he said.

"Where? Is there life after death?"

"I don't know," he said. He couldn't count The Eternal Bar as the afterlife. It was more of rest stop, a waiting place. Beyond those double doors there might be something. Would it be anything like a life with flesh and blood, a beating heart, running on two legs, the pleasure of skin against skin?

He added, "I've been dead for too long."

Margaret tried to reach for him, only to have her hands go through him again. "Adam, why are you waiting? It hurts, I can see it in your eyes."

He wanted a reason for his waiting and standing before Margaret, the disappointment came crashing down on his mind like a brick to the head. The two of them were going in opposite directions. Adam's was death and whatever else was beyond. Margaret's was life, prolonged, stretched into a future he could only dream about. She still had her body, her heartbeat, and the Earth underneath her feet. He looked down at her bare feet, the nails painted purple as if living and breathing was carefree.

The hurt felt like a knife at his spine. He hated to see Margaret alive, robust, with no signs of dying. Then he felt guilty about it and felt himself shrink in front of her.

"Adam," she said, her voice louder, "What's wrong? Where are you going?"

"Ride life for as long as your feet will carry you," he whispered, and felt a sweet gush of relief that maybe he didn't hate her after all. He'd do it too if he'd had the opportunity. Spending time in the bar reliving his life and waiting was no way to live at all.

A tear streaked down her face as she attempted to grab his face with her hands. Since she couldn't touch him, she simply waved her hands there as if she ran them along his cheeks.

"I still miss you," she said.

Then his vision of Margaret became fuzzy and everything went black.

He found himself in The Eternal Bar again, staring at the shot glass laying on its side on the bar top. Fafa stood over him looking concerned and one eye brow was arched as if asking a question.

"Is it time, Adam?" she asked.

"Thank you, Fafa," he said.

For the first time, she touched him by patting him on the shoulder. She picked up the shot glass and said, "You know the way out."

He slid off the bar stool and strolled to the double doors. He pulled on the iron rings and the wooden doors creaked as they opened.

It was a relief not to wait anymore, which surprised him when he stepped into the fog.

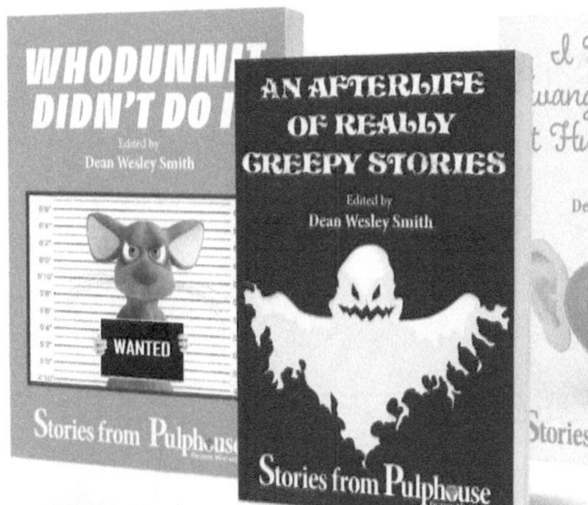

Pulphouse
FICTION MAGAZINE

THE NEWEST COLLECTIONS

pulphousemagazine.com

ROBERT JESCHONEK

Robert Jeschonek continues his streak of being in every issue of this magazine. All thirty-four plus Issue Zero.

The reason Robert has this streak is simply because his stories are often just perfect Pulphouse stories. And with this story, Robert gives this issue a perfect bookend from the Halloween story by Kristine Kathryn Rusch that started the issue.

Robert's stories have appeared in dozens of magazines and he has published dozens of novels as well. He has even worked for DC Comics and early in his career sold me a couple stories when I was editing for Star Trek at Pocket Books. He seems to be able to do it all. And to see all the amazing projects he has done, check out his website at robertjeschonek.com.

TRICK-OR-TREAT IN HELL

ROBERT JESCHONEK

Knock knock knock.

Hands shaking, Boyd Willoughby straightened his red flannel shirt, then slowly opened the door of his cozy little apartment. It was his first trick-or-treat since he'd gone to Hell, and he wasn't sure what to expect.

Just *kids*, as it turned out. Two boys and a girl, ages 6 or 7 or so, waited in the front porchlight, each costumed and carrying a pillowcase as a treat sack.

Boyd blew out a sigh of relief. As far as he could tell, the visitors weren't demons come to terrorize him. Their faces weren't familiar to him, either. If he didn't know better, it could have been a scene straight out of Halloween night back home in Borden, Virginia...except without all the *blood*.

"Trick or treat!" The kids all shouted it at once.

"W-well hello!" Boyd smiled and tried to sound friendly. "L-look at *you* three! A soldier, a cowboy, and a princess."

The kids giggled and held out their pillowcase sacks. As

Boyd turned to get the big bowl of mini candy bars he had found on the table by the door, he took deep breaths, trying to stay calm—wondering when the other shoe would drop.

Because it *had* to, didn't it? This was *Hell*, after all; the satanic welcoming committee at the twisted security checkpoint had made *that* clear.

"Take what you like, kiddos." Boyd shuffled to the door and held out the bowl. For reasons that escaped him, he felt much older and wearier than his actual 63 years and pre-death good health might suggest. Maybe it was just that dying *literally* took it out of him. "Happy Halloween."

Gingerly, the little princess reached into the bowl. As Boyd watched her hand rooting around in those candy bars, a vision of *other* hands suddenly appeared before his mind's eye...*his* hands, drenched with glistening crimson blood.

He shuddered with horror and revulsion. Somehow, he knew, it was a *memory*, a moment in time he'd experienced...though he couldn't remember exactly how or why. All he knew for sure was that he'd experienced that moment on Halloween night—a non-specific Halloween night in an unknown year back on Earth before departing for Hell.

Then, it was gone. The only hand he was watching was the little girl's as it pulled a candy bar in a dark brown wrapper from the bowl.

"Thank you, Mister." She dropped it in her pillowcase, waved, and turned to go.

The kid cowboy grabbed a bar in a red wrapper, and the soldier snagged a yellow-wrapped one. Both boys thanked Boyd politely as they followed the girl off the porch.

"Have a wonderful night, children," he told them.

Standing in the doorway, Boyd waved until they were out of sight down the street. Then, glancing around to make sure no one was looking, he closed the door hard and leaned back against it, shivering.

Since arriving in Hell that day, the only punishment he'd gotten was the slight hassle at the security checkpoint. Otherwise, no demons had jabbed him with pitchforks or flayed the skin from his bones or cooked him alive. But the torture had to come *sometime*, surely. His memories of life on Earth were foggy, but the visions he had of his hands covered in blood on Halloween night were not.

He actually found himself wishing that whoever was in charge of Hell would just get it over with. He was *dead*, but the suspense was *killing* him.

Knock knock knock.

Yelping in surprise, Boyd sprang away from the door when the knock came. Then, he quickly regained his composure and went for the bowl of candy bars again.

"Trick or treat!" hollered the kids when he chucked the door open.

Instantly, he recognized them as the first three kids, but older. Instead of 6 or 7 years old, they were 10 or 11.

They all wore different costumes than before, too. The blond boy was dressed like Davy Crockett, the redheaded boy was a fireman, and the girl was dressed as a doctor, complete with scrubs and prop stethoscope.

They all smiled and were as friendly as before, holding out their pillowcases with no trace of hellish hostility.

It just made Boyd all the more apprehensive.

"Well, don't you all look wonderful!" He pushed the bowl of candy bars forward and gave it a shake. "Help yourselves, children."

The kids were as polite as before, each taking a single candy bar and thanking him.

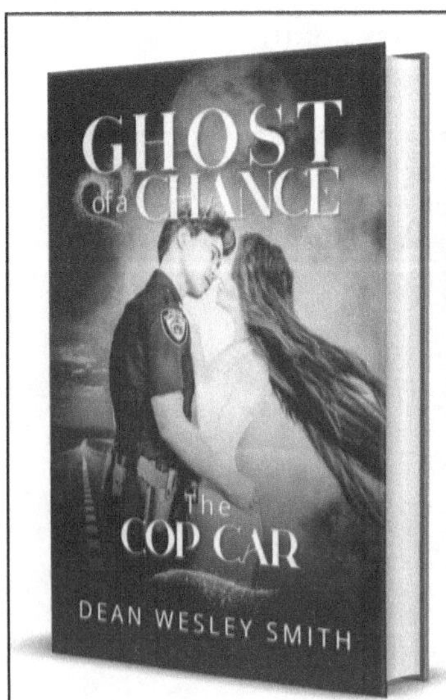

But Boyd couldn't stop looking at their faces and wondering: Did he know them from his life on Earth? Had he *done* something to them? And why were they getting *older* so fast?

"You were here before," he said. "Just a few minutes ago."

The kids looked at each other and shrugged. "I think it might just *seem* that way," said the fireman.

"Sure," said Davy Crockett. "That was a *while* ago. We were just *little* then."

"You live in the n-neighborhood, I suppose?" Boyd returned the candy bar bowl to its spot on the table by the door and wiped his sweaty hands on his bluejeans.

"I live two streets over," said the fireman. "On Anderson."

"My street is Martin," said Davy Crockett.

"And my family lives on Tallman," said the girl.

"I see." Boyd frowned, trying to put the pieces together. "And what did you say your *names* are?"

"Caleb," said the redheaded fireman.

"Tammy," said the girl.

"Austin," said the blond Davy Crockett.

None of the names rang a bell. The significance of the kids' identities, if any, continued to elude Boyd.

"Well, I hope you have a fun night." He managed a weak smile.

Everything was so *normal*, like something out of the world before his death—as much of it as he could *remember*, which wasn't much. There he was in his cozy apartment, the scene of a solitary life...except on Halloween. All of it was so perfectly recreated, so achingly *normal*.

That in itself made him nervous, because he had a feeling it shouldn't have *been* that way in Hell.

Where were the flying demons with the flaming red skin and big bat wings? Where were the piles of entrails rotting in the blistering heat? For that matter, where was the *blistering heat?* It felt as cool as a Virginia Halloween night in that apartment.

"Bye, kids," he said as the three trick-or-treaters wandered off into the night. "Stay safe! Happy Halloween!"

He threw the door shut but didn't lean against it this time. Instead, he crossed the apartment and sat on the edge of the brown leather sofa. It was overstuffed and extremely comfortable.

What kind of hell *was* this?

Combing his fingers through his thin gray hair, he looked around the living room with terror in his eyes. He kept expecting a smoking fissure to open up in the floor, and a hellish denizen to crawl out of it...or the TV to grow a jagged-fanged maw and snap at him like an alligator...or the walls and ceiling to wail and weep blood, oozing and dripping from hideous open sores.

Instead, he just saw the same neat, tidy space. Orange and gold autumn flowers were arranged in a vase on the coffee table. A red apple-scented candle glowed on the end table, and smooth jazz played softly on the stereo. It couldn't have been a nicer place...so why was it in *Hell?* To *lull* him? To give him a false sense of *security* before the *horrors* began?

Or was it all because of something much *worse?*

Knock knock knock.

Boyd stared at the door and wondered who or what was on the other side this time. If he didn't answer it, could he avoid having things turn terrible? On the other hand, if it *was* some fiend finally come to flip his script, at least the *waiting* would be *over.* The feeling of constant *dread* would be gone.

Knock knock knock.

Swallowing hard, he got up from the sofa and walked to the door. He reached for the knob...then *stopped* as the nightmarish vision returned. Once again, he saw his hands before him, drenched and dripping with blood—the crimson color of it so vivid, it could have been happening in the moment instead of flickering before his mind's eye.

The vision lingered for a moment, transfixing him...then faded when a sudden noise broke the spell.

Knock knock knock.

Shaking his head to clear it, Boyd grabbed hold of the knob. He held on to it for a moment, steeling himself for whatever he might find...and then he pulled it open.

"Trick or treat!"

Again, he recognized the three kids—and again, they were older than the time before. At a glance, he guessed they were all in their early teens—noticeably taller and more mature.

"Ah, hello again!" Boyd reached for the bowl of mini candy bars. "How wonderful to see you."

"It's great to see you, too, sir," said redheaded Caleb, who was dressed as a football player.

"You're so nice to us," said Tammy, who wore a superhero costume complete with glittering red tights and a gold tiara. "I always say you make us feel like *we* should be giving *you* treats instead of the other way around."

"Th-thank you." Boyd caught himself blushing. "It means so m-much to hear you say that."

As he'd done twice before, he held out the bowl, and the kids each took one candy bar apiece.

"Hey, Mr. W.," said blond Austin, who was dressed as an astronaut. "Are you all right? Your hands are shaking."

The fear and paranoia were getting the better of Boyd. "I'm fine, I'm fine." Smiling, he plunked the bowl on the table.

"Are you nervous?" Tammy looked worried. "Do you need help?"

"Not at all." Boyd chuckled and waved off her concern. "Just a little chilly, I suppose."

Caleb crossed the threshold and took a step toward him. "Are you sure you're not...*scared?*" He raised his voice and lunged at Boyd on the last word.

Adrenaline blazed through Boyd's arteries, and he jumped. "*Now* I am!" he said, and everyone laughed.

"Well, don't be." Tammy reached into her pillowcase and pulled out a peanut butter cup in an orange wrapper. "You're perfectly safe. You don't have *anything* to worry about." Smiling, she held out the peanut butter cup.

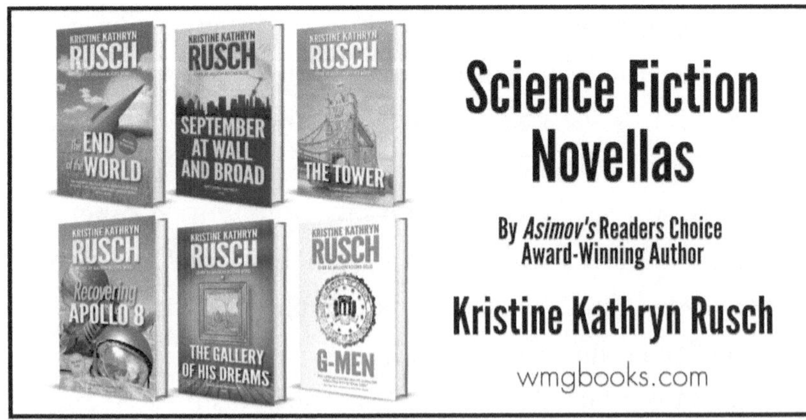

Boyd accepted the candy. "You don't think so?"

"Relax, Mr. W." Tammy gave him a thumbs-up. "You're a good person, and all is right with the world."

"Thank you," said Boyd as they bounded off into the night, waving exuberantly. "You're good people, too."

He stood for a moment in the doorway, expecting the worst to finally erupt. After what Tammy had said, could there be a more perfect moment for all Hell to break loose on him?

Closing his eyes, he took a deep breath of the cool night air. If it was time for him to pay for what he'd done, *whatever it was*, so be it. At least the *waiting* would be over.

Knock knock knock.

"Not again." Boyd went for the candy bar bowl.

Knock knock knock.

He stumbled to the front door and whipped it open.

"Trick or treat!"

Three familiar faces grinned back at him—the same trick-or-treaters as before, but older teenagers now. All of them looked around 15 or 16 years old, taller and leaner and more mature, though they'd only been gone a few minutes as Boyd reckoned time.

Was that what was *happening* here? Did time work differently in Hell than it did on Earth?

Or was there something more sinister at large in the Halloween night wind?

"Here." He held out the bowl of candy. "Take what you like."

"Thank you, sir." Austin was dressed like a hippie, complete with tie-dyed shirt, fringed buckskin vest, and bell-bottom jeans. "I guess you were safe the last time we were here after all, weren't you?"

"I guess so," said Boyd.

"You didn't need to be scared at all." Tammy wore a cute clown outfit, complete with floppy red shoes and a red rubber nose. "We told you so, Mr. W."

"Yes, you did." Boyd was getting impatient. "I appreciate your advice."

"Any time," said redheaded Caleb, who was clad in a Hell's Angels motorcycle outlaw getup. "We like helping good people like you."

"It's not like you're *dangerous* or something," said Austin.

"It's not like you're going to *kill* us," said Tammy, and then she chuckled.

Boyd felt a chill and had another vision of his blood-soaked hands. It disappeared as quickly as it had come. "What do you mean?"

"Nothing, really," said Tammy. "It was just a joke."

Was it? "If you want to *tell* me something, you can just come right out with it, you know," said Boyd.

"What about you?" Caleb cocked his head and narrowed his eyes. "Is there something *you* want to tell *us?*"

"As a matter of fact, yes. There's something I want to *ask* you." Boyd frowned. "Do I know you from *before?* From somewhere other than *this* place?"

Austin shrugged. "Maybe you saw us around the neighborhood?"

"Or in church?" said Tammy.

Boyd shook his head slowly, staring from one of the teens

to the other. "The more I *see* you, the more *familiar* you look to me. But I can't put my *finger* on *why.*"

Caleb cleared his throat and grinned. "Maybe you're better off *not knowing* where you know us from."

Boyd scowled. "And why would *that* be?"

"What if we *remind* you of something you'd rather *forget?*" said Caleb. "Something you've blocked out of your *memory*...and all it needs is one...little...*push.*" He jumped through the doorway and snapped his fingers in Boyd's face.

Then, he threw an arm around Boyd's shoulders and laughed. "Just kidding!"

"*Are* you?" Boyd put down the candy bar bowl. "If there's something I've *forgotten*, you can *tell* me. I promise, I won't be *angry.*"

"There's nothing." Caleb gave Boyd's shoulders a squeeze and unwrapped his arm from around them. "Nothing you need to know."

"If there's anything that might help *explain* what's going on here, *please* tell me." Boyd got another flash of his blood-soaked hands and backed away from the kids. "I don't know how much of this I can *take.*"

"It's Trick-or-Treat on Halloween," said Austin. "What's not to *take?*"

"You're not going to *tell* me, are you?" Boyd almost knocked over a floor lamp as he continued to back away. "But you *know*, don't you?"

"Mr. W? Are you all right?" Tammy entered the apartment, looking concerned. "Can I get you a glass of water, maybe?"

"Just leave," said Boyd. "Take your candy and *leave.*"

"We didn't mean to upset you," said Caleb.

"I'm not upset." Boyd motioned at the door. "Just go, all right? Please, I need some rest."

Tammy looked more concerned than ever. "But maybe you shouldn't be alone, Mr. W."

"I'll be fine. I need to figure this out." Boyd advanced on the kids, making shooing gestures. "I'm turning off my porch-light and lying down now."

"That's okay," said Caleb on his way out. "We won't bother you for a while, sir."

"Yep." Austin waved from the doorway. "At least until *next Halloween*, sir." Turning, he followed Caleb across the porch.

Tammy was close behind. "I hope you feel better," she told Boyd...and then she was back out there, marching off into the night.

And Boyd was slamming the front door shut behind them and switching off the porchlight with a smack of his hand.

Shaking, he crossed the apartment and collapsed on the sofa. As soon as he closed his eyes, another vision of his bloody hands appeared before him...and more. He saw blood on the apartment walls, carpet, and furniture—crimson remnants of some incredibly violent and unknown act.

Whatever he'd done to make that mess—why couldn't he *remember* it? Why did he only see *flashes* of it?

For that matter, how had he managed to make that bloodshed happen at all? What had driven him to commit such *carnage*?

What if it *was* something to do with those trick-or-treating kids? Was *that* why they seemed so familiar? Was it why they kept coming back? Because he'd *hurt* them or *worse* when they'd all still been alive on Earth?

Knock knock knock.

Boyd's eyes shot open, even as he got a sinking feeling in the pit of his stomach. Maybe, if he didn't answer the door, they would just go away.

Knock knock knock.

Knock knock knock.

Or maybe, ignoring it just made it *louder.*

Knock knock knock.

Was this the punishment he was going to face for the violent act he saw in his visions? Eternal knocking and intrusions by murdered trick-or-treaters? He thought he'd almost rather be tortured by demons with pitchforks.

With a grunt, he rolled off the sofa and shuffled to the door. He noticed the porchlight switch was in the *Off* position, where he'd left it—meaning no trick-or-treaters should have been knocking at that point. Boyd's apartment should have been clearly marked as closed for business.

Knock knock knock.

But maybe the rules were *different* in Hell.

Boyd took a deep breath and opened the door. The same three kids were waiting, young adults of 18 or 19 by now.

"Trick or treat!"

"*Enough*," said Boyd. "Enough with the *charade*."

Austin, dressed as a cop, looked at him as if he were nuts. "But we're not *playing* charades, Mr. W."

"That's not what I meant, and you know it," said Boyd.

"We are *literally* trick-or-treating." Redheaded Caleb, costumed as a pirate, shook his pillowcase. Candy wrappers crinkled inside. "*Arrrr*, Matey! Delicious *candy* 'tis our only *mission.*"

"At *your* age?" snapped Boyd.

Austin shrugged. "I guess we're still just *kids* at heart. We love *Halloween.*"

"I'm not *stupid.*" Boyd was getting annoyed. "I can tell there's more going on here than that. I can *tell.*"

"Take a deep breath, Mr. W." Tammy, dressed like an angel this time, crossed the threshold and took him by the elbow. "Let's get you to the couch over there."

Boyd shook her off. At the hint of unfriendliness, the boys pushed through the doorway and took up positions on either side of her.

"Listen to me. *Listen.*" Boyd held up his hands, palms out, in front of him. "I'm *sorry.* Whatever I *did* to you, I'm *sorry.*"

Tammy smiled sadly and shook her head. "You don't need to apologize for *anything*, Mr. W."

"You didn't do anything *to* us," said Caleb. "I *promise.*"

"But I *must* have." Boyd's hands trembled. "You keep coming *back* here."

"To trick-or-treat," said Austin. "You always have the best *candy.*"

"Deny it all you want," said Boyd. "It won't stop me from saying I'm *sorry.*"

"Okay, fine. You're sorry." Austin pointed at the candy bar bowl. "Now can we finally have our *treats?*"

"Does this mean you *accept* it?" asked Boyd. "You accept my *apology?*"

"We don't even know what it's *for,*" said Caleb.

"Mr. W." Tammy stepped closer. "Is there some other reason you think you *did* something to us? Other than the fact that we keep coming back here for trick-or-treat?"

Boyd hesitated. "I've had...*visions.*" His heart raced as he continued. "Visions of something *terrible* I've done."

Tammy cleared her throat. "And the boys and I are *in* these visions of yours?"

He shook his head. "I haven't *seen* you there."

She clapped her hands together. "Then there's no need to *apologize* to us."

"But I don't always remember all the *details,*" said Boyd. "Just *f-flashes*...and *feelings.*" He lowered his hands and frowned. "And I'm starting to get the feeling that you three are *part* of whatever it is I've *done.*"

"Are you trying to *spook* us, Mr. W.?" Caleb sounded amused. "Because that's kind of a creepy story, if you ask me."

"Whatever I've done, I just want to be forgiven." Boyd met the gaze of each trick-or-treater in turn. "I j-just want the *waiting* to end."

"Waiting?" said Austin. "Waiting for what?"

"Payback. Punishment." Boyd winced. "Whatever you're going to d-do to me."

"You've only ever been nice to us, Mr. W.," said Tammy. "Why would we do *anything* to you?"

Suddenly, Boyd had had enough. "I don't *know!* Maybe I *deserve* it! But I'm *begging* you to *forgive* me! Or at least get it *over* with!"

"No offense, Mr. W.," said Caleb, "but I'm starting to think maybe you need *help.*"

"Please." Tammy moved closer and reached for Boyd's shoulder. "You need to calm down."

Boyd shook her off and stormed to the far side of the room, stumbling over the coffee table. "Did it happen on *Halloween?* Is that why it's always *Halloween night,* and you're always *trick-or-treating?*"

"You're not making *sense,*" said Tammy. "Whatever you think *happened* to us, it's all in your *imagination.*"

Suddenly, Boyd grabbed a ceramic statuette of a jack-o'-lantern from an end table and hurled it against the wall, smashing it to orange-colored bits.

All eyes locked on him as he stood there, shaking and flushed. Tears rolled down his cheeks, and he swiped them away.

"I just want to *know.*" His voice was half a whimper. "I want to *remember.* I want to be *forgiven,* or *condemned,* or...*something.*

"And I want this night to be *over.* I want to be *done* with *Halloween.*"

Again, Tammy started toward him...but Caleb caught her by the arm and shook his head. "Let's go."

"Come on," agreed Austin. "I think he needs some time to himself."

Tammy looked like she was wrestling with her conscience. Then, she nodded.

"We're going now, Mr. W." She moved slowly toward the door. "Will you be all right on your own?" When he didn't answer, she just nodded. "Well, take all the time you need to sort this out. Okay?"

Again, he didn't answer.

"All the time you need," said Tammy. "We'll make sure you get it."

Then, she followed the others out of the apartment and shut the door behind her.

As the latch clicked, Boyd let out a deep sigh of relief. At last, he was alone with his thoughts. Maybe he could finally sort things out and get to the truth about his visions.

Or not.

Suddenly, the door burst in without a knock. "Trick or treat!" The three who'd just left crowded back into the apartment.

This time, each of them had to be at least in his or her mid-twenties...and none of them wore costumes.

Unless you counted ratty t-shirts, filthy bluejeans, and track marks all up and down their pale arms, that is.

———

"Mr. W.!" Caleb's eyes were glazed as he stumbled across the room. Whatta you *got* for us?"

"Yeah!" hollered Austin. "Give us something *good*, bro."

Confused, Boyd froze.

"Dude looks *trashed.*" Caleb roared with laughter. "He's all like, *WTF?*"

"Hilarious!" said Austin.

With that, Tammy lurched forward. "You oughtta be *happy,* old man. You *said* you wanted to *remember.* Now that's *exactly* what you're gonna *do.*"

Every warning signal in Boyd's brain was going off at once. A wave of recognition washed over him, but he still couldn't figure out exactly what it all meant.

"We came to see you on Halloween night, remember? Back in the world?" Tammy's blue eyes sparked within the sooty black raccoon circles smeared around them. "Just like this."

Boyd winced and shook his head.

"We *really* needed a *treat,*" said Tammy.

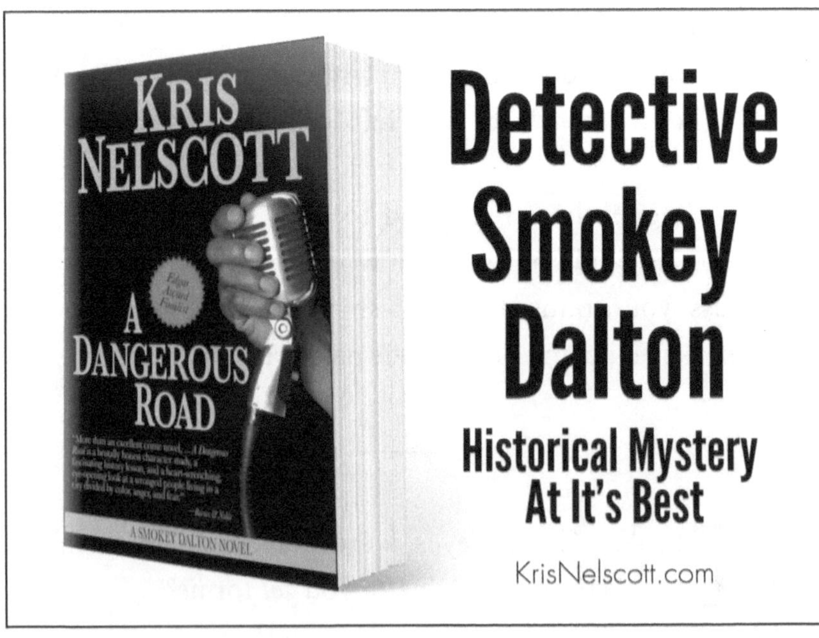

"A very *special* treat." Caleb, still laughing, pretended to shoot his left forearm with a syringe.

"To get it, we needed *cash*," continued Tammy. "*Fast.*"

"Which of course we figured an old dude like *you* would have *loads* of, tucked away," said Austin. "So we *asked* you very nicely to hand it over."

Tammy snorted and scratched her left armpit. "Do you remember what happened after *that*, Mr. W.? Does any of this ring a *bell?*"

Boyd shook his head, shivering.

"You *held out* on us," snapped Caleb. "You said you only *had* a few *bucks* in the apartment."

"*Total bullshit*," chimed in Austin. "Old guys *always* have piles of *cash* in their *walls* and *mattresses* and shit."

"*Then* what happened?" asked Tammy. "Finish the *story*, Mr. W."

"I don't know!" Boyd snapped in frustration. "Did I *do* something...to *h-hurt* you?"

"*That* again?" Caleb laughed. "I swear, you can be *such* a *moron*, Mr. W."

"I don't know what you're *talking* about," said Boyd. "But *whatever* you think I *did* to you, I *apologize!*"

"Like I told you before," said Tammy, "no apologies are *necessary*. *You* didn't do *anything* to *us*."

"Other than *hold out* on us when we totally needed to *score*," said Austin.

"Then *w-what?*" stammered Boyd. "Then *why?*"

"It's not what *you* did to *us*." Tammy's eyes widened as she reached behind her. "It's what *we* did to *you*."

With that, she jerked a semi-automatic handgun out of her

waistband and swung it around, pointing the barrel directly at Boyd.

"*Now* do you *remember?*" she asked as she pulled the trigger, unleashing the thunderous blast of a gunshot.

A round slammed into Boyd's gut, and he crashed to the floor. Searing pain burned through him, blinding him as he clutched at the wound.

Seconds later, his sight flared back to him. Instinctively, he looked down where the bullet had struck.

And saw his hands there, soaked in blood.

Gasping against the pain, he looked around—saw the blood all over the carpet and walls and furniture. It was *everywhere*, just like in his *vision*.

His blood. Not *theirs*.

"I d-didn't...hurt you...after all?" Boyd hissed the words between clenched teeth.

"What was your first *clue?*" Sneering, Tammy blew a wisp of smoke from the gun barrel.

"He's pretty quick on the *uptake*, isn't he?" Caleb laughed.

"B-but...I thought I was in *Hell*...for what I'd d-done to you," said Boyd.

"You got it all wrong, you moron," said Austin.

Boyd clutched at his ruined gut but couldn't stop the blood from bubbling out of him. "Then I'm not being...*punished?*"

"It's more like *we're* being *rewarded.*" Tammy grinned and handed the gun to Caleb. "Don't believe what they told you in *Sunday School. Hell* is like *Heaven* for *sinners.* The worse you *are,* the better you're *treated.*"

"And the three of *us* turned into some *first-class sinners* thanks to the *heroin.*" Caleb aimed the gun at Boyd and curled his finger around the trigger. "So *we* get to relive our favorite *moment* as much as we *want.*"

"B-but why am *I* in Hell...if *you're* the ones...who k-killed *me?*" Boyd gasped and glared at his attackers, wishing he could get up from the floor and lash out at them. "D-doesn't...make *sense.*"

"How should *we* know?" Tammy shrugged.

"Maybe you were secretly a *perv?*" Austin giggled like a lunatic.

"But you won't see *us* complaining. We're tickled pink that you're *here.*"

"Got *that* right." Caleb sneered. "I could keep *this* shit up *forever.*"

He pulled the trigger then, unloading a round in Boyd's chest. Again, Boyd was wracked with blinding pain.

"We practically already *have* kept it up forever," said Austin. "We've been at this so *long,* we can't remember when we *started.*"

"*You* don't remember how long it's been, *do* you, Mr. W.?" Tammy crouched beside him and reached down to pat his head. "Every time we start the game over, it's like the *first day* in *Hell* for you."

Boyd wanted to scream at her, at all of them, but he couldn't force enough breath into his blown-apart chest to get the words out.

"You poor thing." Tammy stroked his bloody, sweat-soaked hair. "I guess the only way you can *stand* going through this again and again is to block out the *memories.* Though apparently those darn *visions* keep reminding you, don't they?"

Boyd choked as his throat filled with blood. He felt darkness closing in, familiar and inexorable...laced with anger at his unjust fate, regret for what the trick-or-treaters had become, and relief for the terrible things he now knew he hadn't done.

Maybe this time, he thought, Halloween night would finally be over for good. Maybe *he* would be over for good.

Relaxing into the darkness, he dared to hope that it would

claim him forever—that there would be *some* justice to the universe, and fate would finally be kind to the murder *victim* instead of the *murderers.*

Knock knock knock.

Then, his eyes fluttered open, and darkness was replaced by the sight of a cozy apartment. Sitting up, he saw no blood on his hands or anywhere else.

Knock knock knock.

The mini candy bar bowl on the table by the door was full. It was Halloween night, his first day in Hell.

Knock knock knock.

Hands shaking, he got up to answer the door.

MINIONS

AT WORK

BOTTOM FEEDERS

BY J. STEVEN YORK

Somewhere off the U.S. Pacific coast...
Helm, status report!
Heading three-four-oh-degrees, twenty knots, Acting Captain Minion No. 1!

PING! PING!
Thanks Number 9! I think I'm getting the hang of this! Pretty fun, even if we're only taking the Naughtyless for an OIL CHANGE!

Incoming fast surface bogey! Reads as the HEROES OF GOOD! Must be their new luxury attack yacht, the HOG Wild!
I thought that was just a TAX DODGE!

KA-BOOM!
Everyone! LEAN CAMERA LEFT!
Depth charge!

The reactor is over-heating, and it looks like they're coming around AGAIN!
DIVE, DIVE! We must lose ourselves in the INKY DEPTHS where they'll NEVER FIND US!

KA-BOOM!
They found us!
Everyone! LEAN CAMERA RIGHT!

This is BAD! We have leaks on decks A, B and D. Also, MINION CAT is wearing a LIFE VEST!
That's it then. We're doomed! It's been great working with you Minions! I only wish...

PING! PING!
Sonar reading some kind of CAVE to star-board, big enough to HIDE in!
Set course! Top speed!

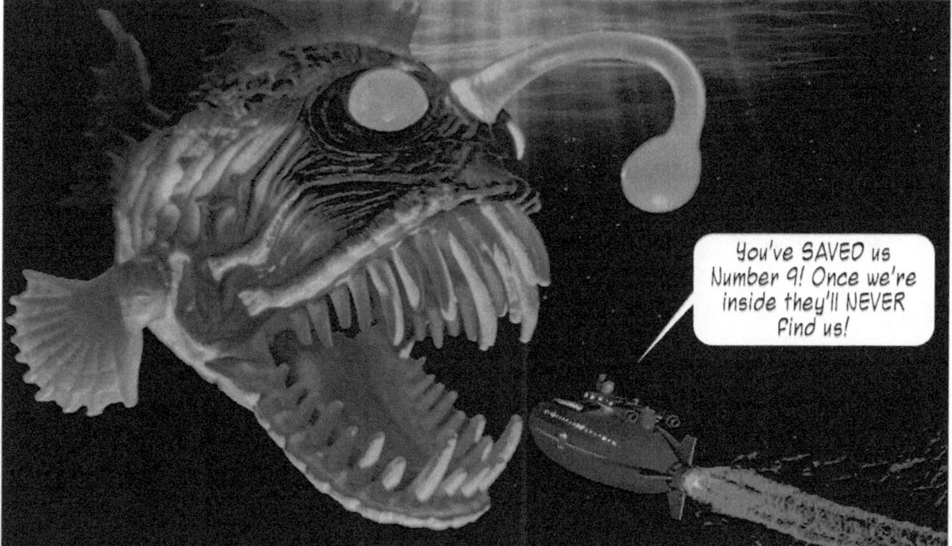

You've SAVED us Number 9! Once we're inside they'll NEVER find us!

www.ingramcontent.com/pod-product-compliance
Lightning Source LLC
Chambersburg PA
CBHW020631110726
47899CB00002B/734